Amanda & Evelyn

Les Chats o...

EIFFEL'S
TRIFLES AND
TROUBLES

AVENTURES EN FRANCE

Laisser les bon temps rouler!

George Arnold

George Arnold
From an Oral Account by
Dr. Buford Lewis, Ph.D.

www.CIAcats.com

EAKIN PRESS ✝ Waco, Texas

Illustrations by Jason C. Eckhardt
Translations by Silvia Ambrosoli Konrad
Typography by Pat Molenaar

This book is a work of fiction, totally
the creation of the author's imagination.
Actual characters, organizations and lo-
cales are used only in a fictional context.
Any similarity to real characters or
events contained in this manuscript is
purely coincidental. However, the cats
and the dogs in the book are real animals who live with the author's family
in Texas.

FIRST EDITION
Copyright © 2011
By George Arnold
Published in the United States of America
By Eakin Press
A Division of Sunbelt Media, Inc.
P.O. Box 21235 ⬧ Waco, Texas 76702
e-mail: sales@eakinpress.com
🖳 website: www.eakinpress.com 🖳
ALL RIGHTS RESERVED.
1 2 3 4 5 6 7 8 9
ISBN 13: 978-1-935632-16-0
ISBN 10: 1-935632-16-7
Library of Congress Control Number 2011927600

Readers React to
Eiffel's Trifles and Troubles

Here's What Students Say

It was very good, very funny, and very believable.

This book was awesome. When I first got it I thought it would be boring because of the elementary level, but as I got into it, I became captivated. This book is good.

It was a great book. It is funny and yet it is educational. It's an easy read, a little lengthy, yet totally worth it.

It is hilarious. I liked it a lot. I also liked that it taught me French.

I think my little brother would LOVE the book; he is nine years old.

Adults Reacted Like This

Fast moving and fun to read.

Arnold has done an outstanding job of combining an interesting fictional story with educational opportunities—a rare feat. The educational opportunities include translations of highly usable French phrases as well as "you are there" insights into locations in Paris.

Great, often spellbinding plot, great characters. Very entertaining and educational because it exposes you to another language and culture. The best book (yet) in the series.

I see this book being enjoyed by kids studying French as well as those not studying the language. Kids can just breeze through the French and keep up with the plot.

This is the best yet of the "Cats In Action" books. Historically accurate, fun to read, and almost believable.

I've read all the C.I.A. (Cats) books, and this is my favorite! I'm ready to book a trip to Paris and who knows? I may bring along my DVD of Ma and Pa Kettle for the flight!

. . . so totally off-the-wall delightful!

I love this story! The kittens are delightful once again.

Carlos the puma is a brilliant sociopath, both in and out of the scene, and I was amazed at the cats' abilities to predict his every move.

. . . a wonderful book to read, and its educational purposes cannot be ignored.

Once again, George Arnold has crafted a fanciful adventure story that parents (and non-parent adults) and children, grandparents, dog or cat lovers can enjoy. Useful for refreshing French vocabulary, too.

For
The English Language Arts teachers
and students at
Bandera Middle School

BOOKS BY GEORGE ARNOLD
From Eakin Press

The Cats of the C.I.A. Fiction Series

Get Fred-X: *The Cats of the C.I.A. (U.S.A.)*

Hunt for Fred-X: *Los Gatos of the C.I.A. (Mexico)*

Fred-X Rising: *I Gatti of the C.I.A. (Italy)*

Tango with a Puma: *Los Gatos of the C.I.A. (Brazil and Argentina)*

Eiffel's Trifles and Troubles: *Les Chats of the C.I.A. (Morocco and France)*

COMING SOON: *München Madness*: *Die Katzen of the C.I.A. (Germany)*

COMING 2013: *Kremlin Capers*: *Koshki of the C.I.A. (Russia)*

Nonfiction books for readers of all ages

Growing Up Simple: *An Irreverent Look at Kids in the 1950s*

Chick Magnates, Ayatollean Televangelist, & A Pig Farmer's Beef: *Inside the Sometimes Hilarious World of Advertising*

BestSeller: *Must-Read Author's Guide to Successfully Selling Your Book*

Detective Craig Rylander clover series with co-author Ken Squier

Enigma: A Mystery

COMING 2011: *UNDERCURRENTS:* The Van Pelt Enigma

COMING 2012: *CONFLICTION:* A Moral Enigma

COMING 2013: THE CHURCH-LADY GANG: A Comic Enigma

For more information, visit the author's Web site:
www.CIAcats.com

Les Chats of the CIA:

Eiffel's
Trifles and
Troubles

Aventures en France

✲ Contents ✲

PART THREE: THE MONUMENTS OF PARIS

PART FOUR: A DOUBLE AGENT

* Author's Note *

Vowels and vowel combinations are pronounced differently in French than they are in English and somewhat differently from Spanish, Italian, Portuguese—the other Romance languages. As you read this book, if you are interested in the correct pronunciation of the French words, please turn to the tables at the end of each chapter and the Glossary near the back of the book. There you will find all the words and phrases along with a guide to help you pronounce them correctly. The pronunciation will be much as you would hear French spoken in Paris.

The symbol (n) is pronounced by closing off your mouth's air passage with your tongue and saying ahh through your nose.

In several places in the book, U.S. dollars are converted to Euros and vice versa. Since the conversion rate floats and the ratio between the two currencies varies from day to day, all comparisons are based on a Euro being worth $1.50 U.S. dollars.

* Cast of Characters *

Luigi: Hilarious tiny orange tabby prankster. Baby brother of Buzzer Louis and Dusty Louise.

 Luisa: Wise, thoughtful and seriously funny little orange tabby. Luisa is Luigi's twin sister.

René Francois Fopaux: First cousin to Buzzer, Dusty, Luigi and Luisa. René is head of the *Brigade Criminelle* of Paris, successor to the famous *La Sûreté Nationale*, model for the F.B.I. as well as Scotland Yard. René is a tuxedo cat like Buzzer. They look identical. The only way to tell them apart is that René wears a dark red *beret*.

Guy G. Gondeaux: Hapless assistant to *René* at the *Brigade Criminelle*, the Paris police detective bureau. *Guy* has his job only because he is related to the president of France's wife's favorite housecat, *Monique Mioux Gondeaux*. *Guy* is all white, hard working, well intentioned and, frankly, a halibut fillet shy of a catch.

Carlos the puma: Infamous international terrorist. A mean motor scooter wanted in seven countries for fire bombings, mass assassinations of government officials and generally creating mayhem.

Supporting Cast

Capitán Ramos: Shady master of a 39-foot river trawler—*El Meteoro*—that carries mail, freight and passengers up and down the long Amazon River. Ramos has thrown in his lot with Carlos, believing the big puma will make him rich. It was Ramos who cleverly aided the terrorist's escape as our story begins.

 Dr. Buford Lewis, Ph.D.: Foreman of Buzzer's little ranching operation in the Texas Hills. The only known Labrador retriever with a doctor of philosophy degree. Buford holds the Rin Tin Tin Chair of Literature and is professor *emeritus* at the University of California at Barkley.

 Bogart-BOGART: Dr. Buford's very smart younger brother and assistant ranch foreman, Bogart-BOGART is often lost in deep thought—a real thinker.

 **Socks**: Gray tabby head of the C.I.A.—Cats-In-Action—which she runs out of the White House basement.

 **Indigenous Rain Forest Tribe**: A group of native hunters from a tribe in Brazil that has never had any contact with the outside world. Led by a chief named Grís.

 Jacques and Georges: French-speaking pilot and copilot of Carlos' Gulfstream G550 executive jet aircraft.

 Anonymous driver: Well-dressed man hired to drive Carlos to Casablanca.

Remy Dewclaux: Head of the French Intelligence Bureau. A German short-haired pointer.

 Count Freidrich von Stuffel: Delusional descendant of Emperor Franz Joseph, the Count hires Carlos to make a big bang in Paris.

 Emile, Franz and Francois: Gypsy team-leader assistants to Carlos in his plan of distraction.

 Gary Gonzachu: An alias for a double agent.

 Captain Marlene: Commander of the fourth company of the *Brigade Criminelle*, an expert on French history.

* Carlos the Puma *
En fruite.
A nouveau[1]

As our story begins, Carlos the puma, international terrorist and mean motor scooter, has just escaped from the
headquarters of the PFA—Policía Federal de Argentina—in
Buenos Aires. After spending only a few hours there following his capture by Buzzer, Cincinnati, Dusty and the twins
Luigi and Luisa, Carlos planted a small bomb made of C-4
plastic explosives in the PFA building.

Capitán Ramos, master of the thirty-nine foot river
trawler *El Meteoro*, smuggled the explosives in to him. In the
confusion following the small explosion, Carlos and Ramos
slipped away to where *El Meteoro* was docked and headed
down the *Río de la Plata* to the open waters of the Atlantic
Ocean, freedom for Carlos and imagined riches for Ramos.

Meanwhile the North American detective team of

---

1. On the Loose. Again.

Buzzer Louis, Cincinnati, Dusty Louise and the tiny twins Luigi and Luisa winged their way in the dancing pig's twin-fanjet Sabreliner from Buenos Aires over the Andes Mountains toward a fuel stop at Guayaquil, Ecuador on their way back to Buzzer's little ranch in the Hill Country of Texas.

About halfway to this first stop, Buzzer received a call on his satellite phone from Socks, head of Cats-In-Action in the White House basement. It seems the C.I.A.'s international satellite had intercepted a cell phone call from somewhere in the South Atlantic to Buenos Aires, and Socks now was sure of Carlos the puma's new destination.

PARIS

1. Les Invalides
2. Champ de Mars
3. Tour Eiffel
4. Trocadero
5. Notre Dame
6. Louvre
7. Musée d'Orsay
8. Grand Palais
9. l'Arc de Triomphe
10. Opera Galleries Lafayette
11. Sacré Cœur
12. Hotel Georges Cinq
13. Hotel Paris Ritz

Part One

Sudden Change of Course

"It's pretty discouraging to spend the better part of a week plotting and capturing that big cat Carlos only to have him manage to escape so quickly. We'll get him again, though. Count on it."

—Buzzer Louis
Retired DO/CIA

* Chapter 1 *
La grande fuite[1]

En El Río de La Plata—Argentina

Capitán Ramos ran his 39-foot trawler *Meteoro* downstream toward the Atlantic Ocean from Buenos Aires—at night and without lights. He had been lucky so far. Taking the C-4 plastic explosives to Carlos the puma at the headquarters of the PFA—Policía Federal de Argentina—in Buenos Aires had been the right thing to do. He was now sure of that. Helping the big puma escape from the authorities would pay off handsomely, he knew. *Carlos is loaded*, he thought, *and now he'll be grateful for my continued help, and he'll share a nice portion of that fortune with me. Soon I'll be rich.*

Ramos' involvement with the international terrorist Carlos the puma had begun only a week ago way up near the head-

---

1. The Great Escape.

* 3 *

waters of the Amazon. Carlos had escaped from a dreadful prison near Brazil's borders with Venezuela and Guyana. The puma had paid *Ramos* a large sum of pesos to bring him to the mouth of the Amazon at the Atlantic. Even though the puma had jumped ship before reaching the ocean, he'd still paid *Ramos* the full amount they had bargained for.

Ramos, in fact, had not known the name or identity of his passenger until hours before Carlos slipped over the side of the *Meteoro* and cat-paddled to the south shore of the big river.

There the puma had made his way to a secret landing strip in the middle of the rain forest and, from there, to Buenos Aires in his quest to get even with a black-and-white cat and the cat's friend, a dancing pig—Buzzer and Cincinnati.

Before Carlos could confront his cat and pig adversaries, however, they had captured him as they worked with the PFA in a clever plot to put the puma back in prison.

Carlos slept below decks. *Ramos* would wait until he woke up to find out where the big cat wanted to go. After all, the major goal at the moment was just getting the trawler to the open waters of the Atlantic without being seen by the authorities.

Ramos knew he was into the thick of things up to his neck. Not even a clever story would save him if the police found Carlos on the *Meteoro*. Still, without allowing himself to lose concentration, *Ramos* began to think of how he could explain having an international terrorist on board if the authorities should confront him. An international terrorist who had just bombed a portion of the headquarters of the PFA—bombed with plastic explosives that *Ramos*, posing as the puma's lawyer, had sneaked into the building in a small suitcase.

* La grande fuite *

Almost silently, the *Meteoro* slid downriver with the current, in total darkness.

* * *

Al Aeropuerto Internaciónal Ezeiza en Buenos Aires[2]

It was six in the morning on the tarmac outside Terminal C at Buenos Aires' big airport. Cincinnati the dancing pig had called ahead. His beautiful twin-fanjet Sabreliner was fueled and ready for the 8,000-kilometer trip back to the Texas Hill Country. Buzzer Louis, black-and-white tuxedo cat and Cincinnati's best friend, was talking softly at the cockpit door with his younger sister, Dusty Louise. Dusty was a pretty gray tabby, who worked hard to overcome her natural tendency to be impatient. Part of her therapy involved learning to fly airplanes. She would help Cincinnati fly the Sabreliner, known as *The Flying Pig Machine*, back home to Texas . . . a long trip with a stop for fuel at Guayaquil, Ecuador.

Buzzer and Dusty's tiny orange tabby twin siblings, Luigi and Luisa, pranksters of the first order who would normally be bundles of energy, slept huddled together under a buckled-up seat belt in the cabin. The capture of Carlos yesterday, followed by his unexpected escape, had made them unusually tired.

Cincinnati, headphones in place, cued Dusty with a hoof pointed toward her as she sat in the right seat of the cockpit. She keyed the microphone clipped around her

2. In Spanish: At *Ezeiza* International Airport in Buenos Aires

chin and spoke to the air traffic controller in the tower to her left.

"Ezeiza ground control, this is Sabreliner seven-zero-niner-niner-alpha bound for *Texas en Los Estados Unidos*,[3] asking for taxi instructions." Dusty knew that all aircraft traffic control worldwide used English to communicate.

"Sabreliner niner-niner-alpha, proceed to runway 11," the controller responded. Wind is from the northeast at six knots. Temperature is sixteen degrees Celsius. There is no traffic in the area, Sabreliner. You're cleared for takeoff. Safe trip."

Cincinnati looked at Dusty Louise. "You take it from here," he said much to Dusty's delight. There was almost no ground traffic this early in the morning and, although Cincinnati knew Dusty was still learning, there was little chance for danger in taxiing to runway 11.

As the Sabreliner roared down the runway and into the sky on its way back to the Hill Country Intergalactic Airport and Buzzer's little ranch in the Texas Hills, Luigi and his tiny twin Luisa woke from their nap and started begging their big brother Buzzer Louis for a story.

"Tell us a story, Buzzy, pleeeze," they asked. "Tell us about you and Cincinnati in Hong Kong when you captured that Chinese opium smuggler, Ar-Chee the Panda."

✳ ✳ ✳

En el Bote Meteoro[4]

Before the sun came up, *Ramos* had the *Meteoro* out in

---

3. In Spanish: Texas in the United States
4. In Spanish: On the Boat *Meteoro*

the open waters of the Atlantic Ocean. He deliberately headed about eighty kilometers—fifty miles—off the Argentinean shore into open water. He wanted to avoid any PFA patrols; no use inviting a boarding. Besides, the sea was calm, and the trawler, with no freight, rode high in the water.

As the morning sun began to peep over the eastern horizon above the softly rolling, glassy surface of the Atlantic, Carlos the puma, escaped international terrorist, woke from his sleep and wandered up from the below-decks cabin. He yawned and stretched casually, as if he didn't have a care in the world.

"Where are we, *Ramos*?" he asked the captain.

"We cleared the mouth of the Río de La Plata about four hours ago, Señor, and we've turned northeast toward Brazil," *Ramos* answered. "I'm staying about eighty kilometers offshore in the open water to be sure we're not searched.

"Where would you like me to take you?" *Capitán Ramos* asked the question that had been burning in the back of his mind all night.

Carlos thought for a minute as if he was doing some time and distance calculations in his head. Then he answered, "Remember the spot on the Amazon where I left your trawler last week?" He recalled his escape as two *Brasilian policía* had boarded the *Meteoro* to look for a big puma who had just escaped from a terrible prison near the big river's headwaters.

Ramos nodded. "I know the spot, Señor, he said with certainty. "I don't think I'll ever forget that spot. I thought we both were goners when the *policía* came aboard."

"*Bueno*,"[5] Carlos said, adding, "Take me there, *Ramos*, only this time closer to the shore. I have friends who'll pick me up there and take me on to my next job. The dratted *Norteaméricano* cat and his pig friend will have to wait. But I'll get them. Count on it, *Capitán*."

Carlos shaded his eyes with his left front paw and gazed out across the open water, adding almost to himself, "Yes, I will get them. Nobody crosses Carlos the puma twice. Nobody!"

For *Ramos*, there was still unfinished business—business that had brought him and the puma to where they were at the moment and where they would be going for the next several hours.

It was time to get down to that business.

"My escape last night was close, Carlos," he said. "I risked much to come to your rescue, no? And now I risk even more smuggling you back to safety. Safety for you. Much danger for me."

Carlos smiled at *Ramos* and said to the captain with a chuckle in his voice, "Why don't you just ask how much I'll pay you for your time and your risks, *Ramos*? Have I not been fair with you to this point? Carlos the puma takes care of those who take care of him. So, *Capitán*, you name your price, and I'll pay it. You know that Carlos has a lot of money, right? And that my next job will pay me even millions more

5. "Good" in Spanish

pesos. Consider the risk to your boat and yourself and your future. And make the price worthy of that risk."

Ramos hadn't expected such a blank check. It confused him, so much so that he changed the subject to give himself time to think. "Where will you go for your next job?" *Ramos* asked Carlos. "Is it somewhere that I can continue to be of service, Señor?"

"Are you looking for a job, *Capitán*?" Carlos asked. "You're a ship's captain. The captain of a fine trawler. A captain with a good business, *Ramos*. If I were you, after tomorrow I would forget I ever met Carlos the puma. Take your new money—how much, again? And keep running up and down the big river."

Carlos hesitated, then added, "Your actions in freeing me from the PFA were frankly reckless. And foolish. I'm grateful, of course. But *Capitán*, you're not cut out to do the kind of work I do."

Ramos cringed. And the price he'd quote the puma went up. A lot.

* * *

In "The Flying Pig Machine" Over Bolivia

"And so, Luigi and Luisa, that's how Cincinnati and I captured Ar-Chee the Panda in Hong Kong. And how I lost a claw from my front paw," Buzzer said, concluding a story that had taken almost two hours to tell as the little Sabreliner flew northwest toward its fuel stop at Guyaquíl in Ecuador.

Luisa looked out the window at the tops of mountains peeping above puffy white clouds.

"Are we there yet?" she asked, causing Luigi to burst into laughter.

"Only kidding," Luisa added, smiling at Buzzer.

Just then Buzzer Louis' satellite phone rang.

"Buzzer Louis," he said. He listened for a minute, saying "Yes" once, and "No" twice and ending the conversation with "Sure. Whatever."

"Who was that?" the ever-curious Luigi wanted to know.

"It was Socks in Washington, Luigi, the head of the C.I.A.—you know, Cats-In-Action. One of you run up to the cockpit and ask Cincinnati if he can come back here for a couple of minutes. We need to talk."

Luisa scampered forward, peeked into the flight deck and, quickly, Cincinnati followed her back into the cabin.

"What's up, Buzz?" the dancing pig asked.

Buzzer answered, "Socks just called. Seems her international monitoring satellite picked up a conversation between a ship somewhere in the South Atlantic and a cell phone in Argentina. Looks like our puma friend may be headed to France. *Parlez vous Francais,*[6] Cincinnati?"

"*Ouí, ouí,*"[7] Cincinnati answered. "Let's gas up in Ecuador and plot a course to gay Paree."

Will Carlos really pay Capitán Ramos *for rescuing him and taking him to safety? Or will he drown the captain and sink the* Meteoro? *Where will the four Texas cats and Cincinnati go after they land and refuel in Guayaquil? Is the big puma really headed for France? What's he planning to do there?*

---

6. Do you speak French?
7. "Yes, yes"

Parlez Vous Francais?[8]

by Cincinnati

Hello, I'm Cincinnati the dancing pig, and I speak perfect French. As we read this amazing story of international intrigue, I'll help you learn some French, too. We'll start with some numbers.

English	French	Say It Like This
one	*un*	A(n)
two	*deux*	DOOH
three	*trois*	TWAH
four	*quatre*	CAHT-reh
five	*cinq*	SANK
six	*six*	SEES
seven	*sept*	SET
eight	*huit*	WEET
nine	*neuf*	NUFF
ten	*dix*	DEES
twenty	*vingt*	VEHN
thirty	*trente*	TROHN-teh
forty	*quarante*	cahr-AHNT
fifty	*cinquante*	sahn-CAHNT
sixty	*soixante*	SWAH-sahn
seventy	*soixante-dix*	SWAH-sahn DEES
eighty	*quatre-vingts*	CAH-trah VEHN
ninety	*quatre-vingt-dix*	CAH-trah VEHN DEES
one hundred	*cent*	SAHN
one thousand	*mille*	MEEL
one million	*un millon*	A(n) mee-YAHN

---

8. Do you speak French?

* Chapter 2 *
Appel à la maison—
Vers l'Est[1]

dans le Meteoro *a Belem, Brasil*[2]

Darkness fell as *Capitán Ramos* slid the thirty-nine foot trawler *Meteoro* beside a dock at Belém on the northeast coast of Brazil, just south of the mouth of the Amazon River. A Shell station sat at the end of the dock. *Ramos* needed to refuel his oversize diesel tanks for the run up the big river to drop off the international terrorist Carlos the puma . . . drop him off on the south shore of the Amazon only a few kilometers from one of Carlos' secret bases in the rain forest, a base with both a mile-long landing strip and a wide circular clearing for helicopters.

Ramos would also take on fresh water and provisions for this run up the Amazon to the headwaters, and he would pick up any freight and mail to be delivered to various

1. Phone Home—Head East
2. In the *Meteoro* at Belém, Brazil

villages along the way. He was resigned to going back to his regular job of delivering passengers, freight and mail up and down the Amazon. There'd be no job with Carlos.

This time there would be no passengers bound upriver, either. The only other soul on his boat would be the big puma, and—with any luck—he would be rid of Carlos by early tomorrow morning.

And he would be rich, or almost rich, with the one million Argentine pesos he would charge Carlos for rescuing the puma from the authorities and delivering him to freedom. On his return from this trip he would sell the *Meteoro*, still a worthy vessel, and invest in a new, larger and faster craft—one that would last until he could retire in ten or fifteen years.

Carlos had slept most of the day on the deck near the bow of the trawler. After all, they had been in international waters. They had seen no other ships, planes or helicopters, and the fresh salt air breeze had been pleasant for a mid-day nap.

As *Ramos* gently nudged the *Meteoro* against the docks by the Shell fuel pumps, Carlos the puma slipped below into the captain's cabin. It would be stupid to have come this far, almost to freedom, only to be spotted and re-arrested.

Carlos turned on his satellite phone and quickly punched in an international number for his secret offices in Tigre, a northern suburb of Buenos Aires. While *Ramos* refueled and took on provisions, mail and freight, the big puma would arrange to be picked up in the morning and taken on to his next job—a job that would pay him more than five million Euros.

Whatever Ramos decides to charge me for this escape, he thought, *it will be small change compared to the millions of Euros I'm about to earn.* Carlos smiled to himself, and then began a conversation as his right-hand assistant answered his call in Argentina.

✷ ✷ ✷

Approchant Guayaquil. Pour fair le plain et planifier la direction[3]

Dusty called the Simón Bolívar airport tower at Guayaquil, Ecuador for landing instructions. "Simón Bolívar tower, this is Sabreliner seven-zero-niner-niner-alpha sixty miles to your southeast requesting clearance to land and refuel."

The answer came quickly. "Sabreliner niner-niner-alpha, proceed to runway two-one. Descend to twenty-five hundred nine miles out and turn to zero degrees. You're cleared to land. Taxi to the Shell sign to refuel. Will you need to deplane, Miss?"

"Yes, Sir," Dusty answered, "and we require the use of a small conference room for an hour or so, if one is available. We are four Texas cats and a dancing pig from Ohio, and we need to conduct an urgent meeting with international conference calls."

"Welcome to Ecuador, Miss," the traffic controller answered. "We'll arrange a small private room for your meeting. Wind is from the northwest at two knots steady. Temperature is twenty-nine degrees Celsius. And the fuel truck is rolling."

---

3. Approaching Guayaquil. For Refueling and Re-routing.

"Thank you, Simón Bolívar tower," Cincinnati responded this time from the left-hand seat in the cockpit. "We'll be on the ground in nine minutes."

It was nearly noon in Ecuador — late morning in the Hill Country of Texas where *The Flying Pig Machine*'s original flight plan was to take them. But with the phone call from Socks about Carlos' likely destination, that flight plan was about to change.

Dusty was sure a change was coming, but she wasn't sure why, or where they might be headed instead of home to Texas.

"Can you give me a clue where we might be going from here, Cincinnati?" she asked the little plane's captain as he made a sharp right turn, spooled back the throttles and pointed the jet's nose down.

"My guess, Dusty, is France," he said. "But that's not for sure. We'll have to call Socks when we get on the ground and see if she has any further idea as to where Carlos might be." Then he added, "Descending to twenty-five hundred with a zero degree heading. You take it from here, Dusty. You can see the runway on the horizon there, and we're about to be lined up."

Dusty was pleased. She was going to land the plane by herself this time, so she quickly forgot about pumping Cincinnati for more clues.

Meanwhile, back in the cabin, Luigi and Luisa stowed their juice-box snacks while Buzzer turned off the video system. After the story about Ar-Chee in Hong Kong, Buzzer had played an old black-and-white movie from the 1950s for the twins—*Ma and Pa Kettle Go to Paris*. When Luisa had asked him why he chose this particular movie, Buzzer only said, "Because it's the funniest movie I ever watched."

Thirty minutes into the movie, Luigi and Luisa had agreed. It was the funniest movie they had ever seen, too. But Buzzer hadn't said a word to them about maybe going to Paris themselves. He'd only suggested they "look for sights you might like to see some day."

So the two of them made a list. Luisa's first choice was the *Eiffel Tower*. Luigi's was the city's famous sewers. "There are probably rats down there," Luigi said matter-of-factly. Buzzer couldn't tell if Luigi thought that was good, or bad.

Luisa knew Luigi would be scared if he actually saw a rat, but she kept that thought to herself. She'd be scared, too.

As Dusty settled the little jet onto runway 21, reversed the thrusters and applied the brakes, Cincinnati spoke through the intercom to Buzzer and the twins.

"We've got a Shell truck to fill our tanks," he said, "and a conference room inside the terminal where we can figure out where we go from here. Just remember, Luigi and Luisa, if you don't go out the street side of the terminal, you won't have to go through customs."

Buzzer turned to the twins. "You two just stick with me. We need you to help us plan, so no wandering around today. *Comprendez-vous, gemeaux?*[4]

Luigi didn't miss the question, and neither did Luisa.

---

4. "Do you understand, twins?"

They immediately looked at each other. "Buzzer just spoke French, Luisa," Luigi said. "You heard it too, didn't you?"

"*Ouí, frère* Luigi,"[5] she said with a smile. "I think that might mean something, don't you?"

"His French sounds better than Pa Kettle's," Luigi said, ignoring his little sister's question. And her French.

* * *

Ramos dit "Au revoir" a Carlos[6]

Ramos cut the diesel engine of the *Meteoro* as he slipped the bow of the trawler near the south shore of the Amazon River. He and Carlos had run most of the night in total darkness, and now it was early morning – just before dawn. And it was time for Carlos to settle up with the captain, making him rich.

"This is where I get off, *Ramos*," Carlos said as he looked over the shoreline to be sure they were exactly where he wanted to go ashore. "So, *Capitán*, how much will you charge me for helping me to escape and bringing me here?" Carlos asked.

Ramos pretended to consider once again the price he would ask. He scratched his chin as if in contemplation. Then he looked at Carlos.

"Carlos," he began slowly, "I have risked much—my entire future as a matter of fact. Your safety just has to be worth a lot to you. And I may still be in danger of being arrested."

---

5. "Yes, brother Luigi"
6. Ramos Says "Goodbye" to Carlos

Carlos, beginning to get impatient, interrupted the captain. "*Ramos*," the puma said, "the time for bargaining is over. I said I would pay whatever you asked. So ask!"

Ramos blurted out his answer, "One million pesos de Argentina for freeing you from the PFA in Buenos Aires, Señor." And then the captain, seeing no reaction from Carlos, added quickly, "And another one hundred thousand pesos for delivering you here to safety."

Carlos smiled. He thought, *Ramos is a better captain than he is a bargainer. I would gladly have paid him twice that amount, but he was afraid to ask too much. That's the very reason I told him he isn't cut out for my kind of work.*

Carlos reached into his fanny pack and pulled out only two bills—a million-peso note and a one hundred thousand peso note. "Thank you, *Ramos*," he said as he handed the money to the captain, slipped over the bow of the *Meteoro* and loped lazily onto the shore and into the rain forest.

Carlos laughed. *The good capitán has more money today than he's ever seen, or will ever see again. But wait until he tries to deposit those big notes. There are going to be questions asked about where he got such big currency. I hope his imagination improves or he may have to launder those bills on the black market for half, or less, their value.*

The big cat laughed out loud and picked up his pace down the path that led to his secret base in the rain forest, 25 kilometers to the south.

Ramos, standing on the deck of his trawler, was—in fact—dumbstruck as he stared at the two bills in his hand. He had never seen a piece of paper money worth more than a thousand pesos before. Slowly he folded the two bills together into a tiny rectangle and slipped them inside the sock on his right foot. He pulled his boot back on. Then, as if hit by lightning, he jumped straight up, clicked his heels, and yelled at the top of his voice, "*Capitán Ramos*, you are rich!"

Carlos, only a few hundred meters down the path from the riverbank, heard *Ramos'* yell and smiled to himself, thinking, *I hope you are right, Ramos. I hope you are right.* And he hurried his steps to be sure he was at the secret base by 10:00, only three hours from now.

* * *

Dans la petite chambre à l'Aéroport Simón Bolivar a Guayaquil[7]

The four Texas cats and the dancing pig sat quietly around a small table in a little windowless room in the airport at Guayaquil.

Luigi and Luisa ate a bowl of Cheerios® each although they both asked for and would have preferred ice cream and chocolate cake for lunch. Dusty nixed that idea immediately.

Buzzer had just closed his satellite phone following a call to Socks in Washington. He turned to the group. "Socks says one of the callers on the

Socks

---

7. In a Small Room at Simón Bolívar Airport in Guayaquil

intercepted call asked the other to 'meet me in the chopper at the usual rain forest base about 10:00 tomorrow morning.' And he also asked to have the Gulfstream flown to Manaus by noon tomorrow for a flight to Paris via Marrakech, Morocco.

"She's pretty sure that means Carlos is headed up the Amazon to a secret base where his helicopter can pick him up in the morning and fly him quickly to Manaus."

Looking at Cincinnati, Buzzer asked, "Does Carlos own a helicopter and an executive jet?"

"A couple of the best, Buzzer," Cincinnati answered. "He bought a French Aerospatiale Dauphin a few years ago—the military version. Then he had it outfitted with a luxurious interior. And we know he owns a Gulfstream G550, quite an airplane. I'm not sure what Marrakech has to do with anything, though. His G550 could fly nonstop to Paris from Manaus easily. Must be something else going on in Morocco."

"That's what Socks thought, too," Buzzer said.

"What are we going to do?" Dusty wanted to know.

To the everlasting delight of Luisa and Luigi who stood and cheered, Buzzer answered, "We're going to Paris. Right away. Today."

"This time we'll be way ahead of him," Luigi offered. "If we leave today, how soon can we be in Paris, Cincinnati? Can I go to the sewers?"

"We'll be there by early tomorrow morning, Luigi," Cincinnati said. "Carlos will still be in the rain forest waiting for his helicopter."

"Can we fly all the way to Paris from Guayaquil nonstop?" Dusty asked the dancing pig.

"No. We'll need to stop once for fuel. My Sabreliner has a long distance pack, but it's no Gulfstream. He can fly higher, faster and farther without stopping than we can. Let's you and I get the charts out and figure out where our stop needs to be."

"We better call Dr. Buford and Bogart-BOGART back in the Hill Country in Texas," Luisa said. "Right now they're thinking we'll be home in another five or six hours. That's not going to happen."

Buzzer handed Luisa his satellite phone. "Good idea, Luisa. You and Luigi go ahead and call them, please."

Luisa looked perplexed. "What shall we tell them?" she asked.

"We'll just tell them what's happening," Luigi said confidently. "We know as much as anybody else in this room, don't we?"

Will Buzzer and the gang really leave for Paris right away? Where do you think they'll stop for fuel along the way? And why is it important for them to get to France ahead of Carlos? Why do you think the big puma wants to stop in Morocco? Will he do something terrible there?

Parlez Vous Francais?[8]

by Cincinnati

Now that you know how to say some numbers in French, *Apprennons les couleurs plus communs.*[9]

English	French	Say It Like This
red	*rouge*	ROO-zh
blue	*bleu*	BLEH
green	*vert*	VAIR
yellow	*jaune*	ZHOHN
orange	*orange*	oh-RANZH
pink	*rose*	ROWS
white	*blanc*	BLAH(n)
black	*noir*	NOWAHR
gold	*or*	OHR
silver	*argent*	ahr-ZAHN
purple	*violet*	vee-oh-LAY
maroon	*bordeaux*	bohr-DOH
brown	*brun, marron*	BRAHN, mahr-ROHN

---

8. Do You Speak French?
9. Let's learn some colors

* Chapter 3 *
La Poursuite commence.
Sur les trois continents[1]

"That's about the size of it, Dr. Buford," Luisa said quietly into Buzzer's little satellite phone. "That smelly puma blasted his way out of the PFA headquarters about midnight last night. Now Socks believes he's headed to France in his big G550 Gulfstream jet, and that he's stopping for some reason at Marrakech in Morocco."

Luigi listened intently to his little twin.

Back at the little ranch in the Hill Country Bogart-BOGART took the phone from Dr. Buford. "That really doesn't compute, Luisa," Bogart-BOGART said. "Why Marrakech? Why Morocco? That G550 could fly all the way From Brazil to Paris with fuel to spare. I think the puma's up to something. Yes, he's up to something, for sure."

---

1. The chase is on. On three continents.

Dr. Buford spoke up. "Can Cincinnati's Sabreliner make it to France from Ecuador?"

"No way," Luigi said. "We have to stop somewhere along the way for fuel. But remember, Dr. Buford, we'll have almost a full day's head start on Carlos. He can go higher and faster than we can, but we'll be there waiting for him, thanks to Socks' satellite."

"Good luck, guys," Dr. Buford said. "Call us when you get to France. Goodbye, now."

"*Au revoir*, Dr. Buford and Bogart-BOGART," Luisa said. "*Nous arriverons bientôt a la maison.*" [2]

Meanwhile, Dusty Louise, Buzzer Louis and Cincinnati had their desktop keyboards clicking as they pored over charts spread out on the opposite end of the table. Cincinnati was scratching his chin. "There's just a lot of water between here and the west African coast," he said to nobody in particular. "And there are some places on the Atlantic coast of Africa I'd rather not stop. Not safe. Hmmm."

Dusty was clicking furiously through World Mapper on the Internet. She looked up, smiling like the cat that ate the canary. "Dakar in Senegal is only 3,300 miles from here. That's 5,300 kilometers. We could easily make that."

Then she turned to Cincinnati. "Of if you're up for testing your long distance pack, there's always Marrakech in Morocco. That's airport symbol GMMX, and it's a little less than 4,200 miles—6,700 kilometers. We could do that couldn't we, Cincinnati?"

---

2. "Goodbye. We'll be home eventually."

"Either one's okay with me," Cincinnati said, then to Buzzer, "Marrakech will take about eight hours. Dakar would take only about six and a half. Do you think the twins can possibly sit still for a full eight hours?"

Buzzer smiled. "With a story or two and another look at *Ma and Pa Kettle*, I'll bet they'll be fine. They're not old enough yet to know much difference between six and a half and eight, anyway. Since Carlos seems to be stopping in Marrakech, what could it hurt to nose around the airport a bit while our plane's being refueled?"

Another thought seemed to strike him. "How far is it then from Marrakech to Paris?"

Dusty clicked her keyboard hurriedly. "Looks like a little more than 1,100 miles, Buzz. Maybe two hours, Cincinnati?"

"Make it two and a half to be safe—about the same as Ohio to Texas," the dancing pig said.

"Marrakech it is, then," said Buzzer.

As the conversation about stopover destinations ended, Luigi and Luisa wandered up and Luisa said, "What language do they speak in Morocco?"

Cincinnati answered, "*Il parlent français la' bas, Luisa.*"[3]

"*Peut quelqu'un de vous parler français?*" Luigi asked.[4]

"*Ouí ie parles français très bien,*" Cincinnati said. "*Et Buzzer aussi en effect.*"[5]

Dusty looked confused. "What did you just say, Cincinnati?

---

3. "They speak French there, Luisa."
4. "Can any of you speak French?"
5. "Yes, I speak French very well. And so does Buzzer."

"He said he speaks French very well, and so does Buzzer," Luisa answered.

Dusty was furious. She thought, *How can those two little kittens understand French? They've never heard a word of it before. Paris is not going to be fun for me if they keep that up.* She sighed and went back to her laptop to print directions for the flight.

"I'll file a flight plan," Cincinnati said. "*Veux tu m'aider, Dusty?*"[6]

Luigi started to translate, "he said, 'Do you want to help me, Dusty.'"

"Don't you start translating for me, Luigi!" Dusty said. "You, either, Luisa."

Luisa leaned over to Luigi. "Dusty's in a snit. Let's go get an ice cream and stay clear of her."

As the twins scampered out, headed for the snack bar, Cincinnati went to work on his laptop, preparing the flight plan to Marrakech. And then on to Paris.

✱ ✱ ✱

Dans la forêt de pluie dans le grand fleuve de l'Amazon[7]

As Carlos rounded a bend in the familiar trail near his

_____
6. "Want to help me, Dusty?"
7. In the rain forest south of the big Amazon River

base in the rain forest, he heard the unmistakable pop-pop-pop of helicopter rotor blades in the distance. *Great,* he thought, *my Dauphine is almost to the base, and so am I. We'll pump some jet fuel into the tanks from the barrels behind the shack, and we'll be out of here for the short hop to Manaus in less than an hour.*

Ever fearful of betrayal, Carlos crept behind the little green storage building he called a "shack" to watch as the helicopter hovered above the 40-meter-wide landing pad and dropped slowly, settling lightly on the ground. As the rotors would down, he saw the two men he expected to see jump down from the graceful airship and move slowly across the clearing to the shack. Satisfied everything was safe, Carlos stepped out to greet them.

The taller man, the pilot, saw Carlos and greeted him in his native Spanish. *"¿Qué pasa, Carlos?"*[8]

"Todo es bien,"[9] Carlos answered. "Let's get some fuel on board so we can get on over to Manaus by noon. Is my Gulfstream on its way there?" he asked the smaller pilot.

"Sí, Señor,"[10] the copilot answered. "I was able to get *Jacques* and *Georges* to fly you to France as you asked.

"Un bon travail, Ramón,"[11] the big puma answered. "Having them along will give me the chance to sound like a French native again. After four years in prison, I'm not sure the accent's as it should be."

As the helicopter pilots stretched a long hose from barrels of jet fuel stored behind the shack and attached it to

---

8. "What's happening, Carlos?"
9. "Everything's fine."
10. "Yes, Sir."
11. "Good work, Raymond." In French.

the Dauphine's fuel tank, Carlos thought of an errand he wanted the two of them to take care of. "After you drop me off at the airport in Manaus, stop back by here. Bring a couple of barrels of jet fuel with you. In fact, let's stow these two empty barrels," Carlos said, pointing to a couple that lay on their sides next to the shack. "You can fill them up in Manaus and drop them by here on your way back to Buenos Aires."

He scratched his left ear. Then added, "Let's always be sure we have at least two full tanks for the Dauphine on hand here. You never can tell when we might need fuel in a hurry."

"I have a question for you, Boss," the tall pilot said. "Two questions, in fact. If I don't need to know, don't tell me, of course." He looked at Carlos, and seeing no reaction, he went on, "Why not have the Gulfstream pick you up here? The strip is plenty long to land and take off."

Carlos glanced down the mile-long landing strip for fixed-wing aircraft before he answered. "These plants and vines grow so fast here I wasn't sure if the surface growth might be too dense for my airplane. There wasn't time to scrape the strip. And remember, I paid almost 150 million pesos for that Gulfstream. No sense in risking an accident or even minor damage. Besides, the Dauphine doesn't mind a few ferns and weeds." He waited a moment, then said, "Did you have another question? You said two."

"Jacques said you were stopping in Marrakech on your way to Paris. We're just curious about that, knowing your Gulfstream can fly nonstop, we wondered why the stop in Africa?" the pilot asked.

"Sorry," Carlos said. "That I won't answer. Neither you nor *Ramón* needs to worry about that right now. In fact, neither do *Jacques* or *Georges*. The two of them will find out in due time and I'm sure they'll tell you when they get back. Which reminds me, I want us to cut out the international phone calls for the next few days unless there's a big emergency. Somehow, I suspect our voice calls are being overheard. It's just a feeling I have. So use only the secure scrambler in the office in Tigre if you urgently need to talk to me. If I need you, I'll call from the secure phone in the Gulfstream."

Fuel tanks on the gleaming Dauphine now full, the pilots stowed the hoses and hand pump, climbed into the cockpit and started the two jet engines.

"Next stop, Manaus," Carlos said as he settled into one of the soft leather recliners and buckled his seat belt.

The Dauphine lifted straight up above the treetops. Its nose dipped and its tail swung to the right as it climbed and headed northwest toward Manaus and the big jet that would take Carlos first to Africa, then on to Europe.

* * *

A l'aéroport de Guayaquil. A nouveau.[12]

Buzzer spoke into his small satellite phone. "Yes, Socks. We're headed to France. We'll leave here in a few minutes bound directly for Marrakech in Morocco for refueling. Cincinnati and I intend to snoop around a little at the Marrakech airport to see if there are any clues as to why Carlos is stopping there. We should get to Marrakech about

---

12. At the airport in Guayaquil. Again.

9:00 tonight your time and then to Paris by early tomorrow morning."

He listened a minute, then said, "What's that? What do you mean? Yes, it's about 4,200 miles to Marrakech. That's within Cincinnati's Sabreliner's range. No problem. Then it's another 1,100 miles or so to Paris. We've decided to touch down there at *Le Bourget* Airport a few miles north of Paris instead of the bigger airports. That's where Charles Lindbergh landed in 1927, you know. When he made the first trans-Atlantic flight ever in *The Spirit of St. Louis*. "We'd like to be as invisible as possible once we get to Paris."

Buzzer continued, "We should be there at least twelve hours ahead of Carlos. And we'll be staying at the *Georges Cinq Hotel* downtown. Could you wire us maybe five thousand Euros for incidentals? Once we set up contact with the *Sureté*, Cincinnati or I will FAX you the paperwork to bill the French for at least part of our expenses."

Buzzer listened again. "Right, Socks," he said. "The old *La Sureté National*[13] is now *La Brigade Criminelle*,[14] but guess what? My first cousin is the new head of it. That's right.

"His name is *René Francois Fopaux*. We'll get all the cooperation we need. Funny thing is we look identical. Even you couldn't tell us apart. Except he always wears a red beret. And his assistant is no super hero, I can tell you that. He's a white longhaired cat named *Guy G. Gondeaux*.

"*René* tells me *Guy* tries hard, but he's a halibut short of

---

13. National Security (Early French national police force)
14. The Criminal Brigade, successor to *La Sureté*

a catch, if you know what I mean. Still, he keeps his job because his sister is the favorite housecat of the French president's wife. The sister's named *Monique Mioux Gondeaux*. Funny, huh?"

Again Buzzer listened to his boss in Washington, D.C. "Right Socks, and if you see the president, give him my regards. And Cincinnati's. We'll call you tomorrow morning, your time. *Au revoir*."[15]

"All set?" Cincinnati asked.

"*Je suis prêt*,"[16] Buzzer answered.

"Then we're off to Marrakech," Cincinnati said. "Last one on the plane's a smelly puma!"

Buzzer and Cincinnati looked around the room. There was nobody else there. As they walked into the terminal building they saw through the big windows that Luigi and Luisa were waiting on the stairs to *The Flying Pig Machine*, and Dusty was scurrying toward the stairs carrying maps and charts under her right arm.

Buzzer smiled at his dancing pig friend. "Looks like one of us will be that smelly puma," he said.

Why do you think Carlos wants to stop in Marrakech? Will Buzzer and Cincinnati figure out why when they stop there hours ahead of the big puma? Will Cincinnati's little jet have enough fuel to cross both South America and the Atlantic Ocean without stopping? And what about Luigi and Luisa? Can they possibly make it through an eight-hour flight?

---

15. "Goodbye."
16. "Ready."

Parlez vous Francais?

by Cincinnati

Numbers and colors are a good start toward learning some French, *mais maintenant c'est le moment de apprende les jours de la semaine et les mois et saisons de l'année. C'est facile, n'est pas?*[17]

English	French	Say It Like This
Sunday	*Dimanche*	di-MONZ
Monday	*Lundi*	lawn-DEE
Tuesday	*Mardi*	mahr-DEE
Wednesday	*Mercredi*	mair-creh-DEE
Thursday	*Jeudi*	zhu-DEE
Friday	*Vendredi*	von-veh-DREE
Saturday	*Samedi*	sahm-DEE
January	*Janvier*	zhon-vee-AY
February	*Févrevi*	fev-ree-AY
March	*Mars*	MAHRS
April	*Avril*	avh-REEL
May	*Mai*	MAY
June	*Juin*	ZHUEN
July	*Juillet*	zhu-YAY
August	*Août*	OOT
September	*Septembre*	sep-TAHM-brah
October	*Octobre*	ock-TOH-brah
November	*Novembre*	noh-VAHM-brah
December	*Décembre*	dee-SAHM-brah
Spring	*Printemps*	prin-TAH
Summer	*Été*	ET-ay
Fall	*Automne*	ah-TOH(n)
Winter	*Hiver*	ee-VAIR

---

17. But now it's time to learn the days of the week and the months and seasons of the year. It's easy. Right?

* Chapter 4 *
De l'eau, de l'eau ... Partout[1]

Dans l'appareil "Cochon Volant" à l'aeroport de Guayaquil[2]
When the fuel tanks were full and the flight plan filed, Cincinnati gave Dusty the go-ahead to start the engines of his little plane and to contact the tower for taxi and takeoff instructions.

"Guayaquil tower, this is Sabreliner seven-zero-niner-niner-alpha ready for takeoff bound for Marrakech and on to Paris," Dusty spoke into the little microphone clipped under her chin.

"Sabreliner niner-niner-alpha, taxi to runway two-one. Cleared to Marrakech as filed. Fly heading zero two one. Climb and maintain one zero thousand. Leaving two thousand, contact Guayaquil Departure on 123.9. Wind 310 at two knots. Temperature is thirty-one degrees. Cleared for take-off. *Bon voyage, Mademoiselle,*"[3] came the response from the tower.

---

1. Water, Water . . . Everywhere
2. In *The Flying Pig Machine* at the Airport in Guayaquil
3. "Safe trip, Miss."

It was 2:00 in the afternoon in Guayaquil as Dusty sent the little Sabreliner barreling down the center of runway 21 and turned northeast in a steady climb. It would be 1:00 P.M. back in the Hill Country and early evening in Marrakech and Paris.

Dusty turned toward Cincinnati in the left seat of the little jet's cockpit. "We've got a ways to go, Cincinnati. What's your preferred altitude once you talk to Guayaquil Control?"

"Let's take her up to 31,000, Dusty. We should pick up some tailwinds, and after we burn off some fuel, we'll go up to 37,000 so we won't have to worry about having enough fuel for 4,200 miles," Cincinnati answered, adding, "and eight hours."

Meanwhile back in the cabin. Luigi and Luisa had begun their favorite airplane game. They called it "jumpseat." Perching atop a seatback, they would leap to the next seatback. Around and around the cabin they'd go, yelling "Ribbit" with each leap. As long as the flight was smooth, Buzzer tried to ignore their commotion. After all, it would soon tire them out, and he wanted them to sleep during at least part of the eight-hour flight to Marrakech. *There's not much to see out a window over the Atlantic, even in the daytime*, he thought.

After their fourth "Ribbit-ing" trip around the cabin, the twins climbed into big brother Buzzer's lap and began to beg for another story.

"Tell us about the last time you were in Africa," Luisa said.

"Yes, Buzzy, tell us about you and Cincinnati when you captured Ahmed the stick. Remember? Cincinnati pretended to be a pulled-pork sandwich, didn't he? Tell us again. I've forgotten," Luigi begged.

"Then can we watch *Ma and Pa Kettle* again? Pleeeze!" Luisa chimed in.

"Did you and Cincinnati catch Ahmed the stick in Morocco, Buzzer?" Luigi asked.

"No, Luigi, it was in Ethiopia, way on the other side of Africa," Buzzer smiled. He'd told the twins this story at least a dozen times, and he knew they knew every word of it and could recite it to him. But they loved their stories, and they had eight hours to kill before they'd be back on the ground.

"Okay, you two. How about a story, then a nap, then *Ma and Pa Kettle*? Will that work for you? Will you take a nap after the story?" Buzzer asked.

"You won't play the movie until after we take a nap, will you Buzzy?" Luigi had this little game all figured out.

"Right," Buzzer said. "So what's it going to be?"

"A story, a nap—we promise—and then *Ma and Pa Kettle*," Luisa said, batting her eyelashes and cocking her head at her big brother. This was her "cute" pose, which she knew Buzzer couldn't resist.

"Are you good with this plan, Luigi?" Buzzer asked. He had to be sure both twins bought into the nap business. They always had to do things in unison—never one at a time.

Luigi saluted. "Yes Sir, Sir! A story, a nap and then a movie. I'm cool with it." Luigi spoke as if reporting in to a new duty station.

Buzzer began, "Once upon a time about three years ago, Cincinnati and I were in Brussels. Well, Cincinnati was in

Brussels, actually, and I was in Rome, when that clever Ethiopian terrorist Ahmed the stick suddenly reared his head. We had to move fast. Cincinnati grabbed a NATO jet fighter to get from Brussels to Rome in a hurry . . ."

Buzzer was interrupted by the sounds of tiny twin buzz saws. Luigi and Luisa had already fallen asleep in the seat next to him. Buzzer gently buckled a seat belt around them, pulled down the window shade above his left shoulder and closed his own eyes. This was a good time for him to take a nap, too.

✱ ✱ ✱

Dans la forêt de pluie, une fois de plus[4]

Carlos was not a happy puma. Engines of his *Hélicoptère Dauphine*[5] had begun to falter and spin erratically shortly after the sleek ship had lifted off for the short hop to Manaus. *Ramón*, his co-pilot, had immediately suspected the barrel of fuel they had used to fill the tanks might have been tainted, probably by a lot of water.

While the lanky pilot was pulling a sample of fuel from the Dauphine's tanks, the co-pilot examined the barrel they had used to refuel the helicopter a few minutes earlier.

"Water in here," the pilot reported. "What a mess! How could that happen?"

"I've got water residue in the bottom of the barrel, too," *Ramón* reported.

"Well, rats! Nothing to do but drain the tanks and hope the two remaining barrels don't have water in them," Carlos

---

4. In the Rain Forest Once Again
5. Dauphine helicopter

said. "We don't need a lot of fuel to get to Manaus. I've been meaning to get an above-ground tank put in here so we wouldn't have to fool with hand-pumping from barrels. As soon as I get back from this next job, I'll do that for sure. Meantime, *Ramón*, how do those last two barrels look?"

Ramón had sampled both and reported there was no water on the bottom—a pretty good sign that the fuel would be safe to use. The co-pilot turned to his associate. "Let's empty those tanks and put in these two barrels. That ought to do it," he said.

While the pilot and co-pilot were replacing the jet fuel, Carlos wandered a ways down the path toward the Amazon. Suddenly he looked up and there, standing in front of him, was a group of indigenous native Americans, the same group he had encountered only a week ago on his way from the big river to the landing site. Their chief was named *Grís*, and Carlos had given them a Bic® lighter—to them a magic fire stick.

Now here they were again. *Grís* smiled to show he meant no harm, Carlos guessed, and the chief stepped forward with his hand out, palm up. In the hand was the little disposable lighter Carlos had given him only the week before. *Grís* tried to light it several times, but there was no flame. He looked confused, perplexed even, as he handed the Bic to Carlos. The big puma tried to light it several times. "This thing's out of gas," Carlos said, although he knew the chief and his companions wouldn't understand what he was saying.

Carlos reached into his fanny pack and pulled out two more lighters. He struck each one, showing the *Indios* that these fire sticks worked. Then he handed them to *Grís*, who bowed in apparent gratitude.

The chief took Carlos' paw and began to lead him toward the clearing. He led the puma directly to the back of the green shed where the fuel barrels were stored. *Grís* pointed to an empty barrel as another member of his group handed him a big gourd full of water. Instead of drinking the water, the chief tipped the gourd and poured the water into the barrel. He motioned with his left hand inside the barrel, moving it from halfway down inside to the top, palm down.

There it was! The natives had thought the barrels were full of water and had filled the only one that had been opened—one whose top they could get off. And they had filled it to the top to be helpful, to repay the kindness Carlos had shown them with the gift of the lighter.

It made no sense to Carlos to try to explain anything. He didn't understand their language, and they couldn't understand him. So he just smiled and bowed in a "thank-you" gesture.

Armed with their two new fire sticks, the indigenous group turned and sprinted back up the trail. After ten or so steps, they stopped, turned and bowed their foreheads to the ground. Then they rose and disappeared into the rain forest, just as they had a week ago.

Carlos thought, *There's a lesson here if I could find it. But I still think being nice to them will pay off in the long run. In spite of a barrel of ruined jet fuel and an hour or so delay. Ramos proved my theory: Be nice to someone and that kindness will come back when you need it most.*

Carlos and the Dauphine lifted off again headed for Manaus, the big puma's Gulfstream G550 and a flight to Marrakech.

* * *

Dans l'air au dessus de Trinidad et Tobago.[6]

Luigi woke from his nap slowly. He'd been asleep for more than two hours, and so had Luisa who, in fact, was still asleep.

Luigi poked at his little twin sister with a front paw. Then he shook her gently. He wanted her to be awake, too.

She opened one eye and looked at him. "Are we there yet?" she asked with an immediate grin.

"Not yet. Maybe in five or six more hours. Where's Buzzer? Luigi asked."

"I don't know, Luigi. I've been asleep, remember? You're the one that's awake. Where did he go?"

"I just woke up, myself," Luigi said, rubbing his stomach. "And boy, am I hungry."

"Me, too. Wait just a minute."

Luisa hopped down and scampered forward to *The*

---

6. In the Air over Trinidad and Tobago

Flying Pig Machine's small galley. She heard Buzzer, Dusty and Cincinnati talking softly inside the cockpit. However, hunger pangs overcame her natural curiosity about their conversation. She pulled open a cabinet door and grabbed two pre-packaged granola bars. One in each front paw, she went quickly back to the seat she and Luigi had shared while they slept.

Handing one of the snacks to Luigi with a grin, she said, "Here you go, little brother. I just made these myself. In the microwave up there in the galley. I hope you like them." She unwrapped her bar, "And, by the way, Buzzer's in the cockpit with Cincinnati and Dusty. I couldn't hear what they were talking about."

Luigi ripped off the cellophane wrapper and took a big bite of the granola bar just as Buzzer walked back down the aisle, followed by Cincinnati.

Still chewing a raisin and a cashew nut, Luigi looked at Luisa. She knew by the way he rolled his eyes and shook his head that he was about to go into one of his acts.

In a slow and raspy high-pitched voice Luigi said to her, "You shore are a good cooker, Ma. This is cuisine fit fer a Paris bistro. And you made it so fast."

Luisa laughed and went into a gravelly-voiced character herself. "Don't you be a-trying to butter me up none, Pa. You're still in trouble with me fer lettin' that hotel bellboy say I's too fat for this place's tiny little elevator. Made me come upstairs here by m'self."

Cincinnati and Buzzer stood and watched this little drama unfold. The dancing pig looked at Buzzer and shrugged with a questioning look on his face. Buzzer held one paw up in the air and mouthed silently, "Just wait a minute. This might be funny."

"Well, Ma, I thought he's a bein' a little bit rude all right, but the truth is we couldn't all three fit in that little birdcage, could we? Not with our suitcases and all," Luigi said.

"You should'a let him have what fer, Pa. Besides, we kin carry our own suitcases. It's not like they's very heavy is it? What'd we need that little pipsqueak for, anyway? Just so's he could hold out his hand, pretend he did us some great favor and wait 'til you put summa them French franckies in it."

"Maybe he's just a bit of a beggar, Ma. Might'n he have twelve kids and a sick wife at home needin' some vittles? You shore could whip up a tasty mess for 'em, Ma. Then maybe you could hold out yer hand to get summa those franckies back? 'Cause you shore are a good cooker. Yes indeed you are, Ma," Luigi continued.

"I got twelve kids at home m'self, Pa. An' you make a baker's dozen fer me. You don't see me goin' 'round with my hand out spectin' some kinda reward fer doin' not much a nothin' do you?"

Luigi couldn't keep it up. He burst into uncontrollable laughter, followed immediately by Luisa, who was nearly hysterical. They rolled around their seat clutching their sides and laughing until tears ran down both their faces.

Cincinnati still didn't understand the meaning of their dialogue, although he joined in the laughter with Buzz and the twins.

"Let me guess, guys," Buzzer said. "You were Ma and Pa Kettle in Paris. Right?"

"Bingo!" Cincinnati said. "I knew I'd heard those lines and voices. A long time ago, it was. But you two are pretty good mimics."

"Can we have our story now, Buzzy? Huh? The one about you and Cincinnati and Ahmed the stick in Etheropia?" Luisa asked.

"That's Ethiopia, Luisa," Cincinnati said. "And I don't much like to remember that story. I almost got turned into a North Carolina pulled pork barbecue sandwich that day."

"I'll tell you the story since you both did take your naps," Buzzer said. "Then we'll watch the real Ma and Pa Kettle again."

Luisa smiled. Luigi stood and saluted Buzzer, but he stood so fast he toppled over backward. And that started another round of hysterical laughter.

Cincinnati said, "I'm going back to the cockpit. At least these two are in their usual happy mood. Good storytelling Buzzer. And don't forget to save me from Ahmed and his henchmen at the end. I still don't care for barbecue sauce or fire pits." Cincinnati smiled, then turned and walked back to the cockpit to see what Dusty Louise was up to.

Do you think Carlos' helicopter will have enough good fuel to take him to Manaus? Will the indigenous native tribe keep filling the jet fuel barrels with water? Could that cause the helicopter or Carlos' Gulfstream to crash? When will the four Texas cats and Cincinnati get to Marrakech? Will they have to stop for fuel before they get there? Have you ever seen a Ma and Pa Kettle movie? Did you think it was funny?

Parlez Vous Francais?
by Cincinnati

Now that you know your way around the calendar, *nous allons apprendre quelques paroles et phrases utiles.*[7]

English	French	Say It Like This
thank you	*merci*	mare-SEE
you're welcome	*de rien*	duh-RRIE(n)
hello (greeting)	*bonjour*	bohn-ZHOOR
hello (answering the phone)	*allo'*	ah-LOW
goodbye	*au revoir*	aw-REVWAH
good/well	*bon, bien*	BOH(n), BYIN
very good	*très bien*	TRAY BYIN
please	*s'il vous plait*	seel voo PLAY
at your service	*a votre service*	ah VOH-treh sair-VEESE
I want to introduce you to	(FORMAL) *je veux vous presenter a*	zhuh vuh voo pray-szin-tay ah
	(FAMILIAR) *je veux te presenter a*	zhuh vuh tuh pray-szin-tair ah
Sir	*Monsieur*	meh-SURE
Ma'am	*Madame*	mah-DAHM
Miss	*Mademoiselle*	MAHD-mwah-szell
What time is it?	*Quelle heure est-il?*	kell air eh-TEEL?
Where are we going?	*Ou' allons nous?*	oo ah-LOHN noo

---

7. We're going to learn some useful words and phrases

Ready?	Prêt?	PREH?
Let's go!	Allons!	ah-LOHN!
okay, good, sure	bien, bon, sûr	bee-IH(n), BOH(n), SEUR
more slowly	plus lentement	pleu LAHN-teh-MAH(n)
faster	plus vite	pleu VEET
How's it going?	Comment ça va?	Coh-MOH(n) say vah
maybe, perhaps	peut-être, c'est possible	PET-etreh seh poh-SEE-bleh
Do you speak English?	(FORMAL) Parlez vous anglais?	pahr-leh voos ahn-GLEH
	(FAMILIAR) Parles tu anglais?	pahr-leh teu ahn-GLEH
I don't speak French well.	Je ne parle pas bien français.	zhuh nuh PAHR-leh pah bee-IH(n) FRAHN-say
Where is a telephone?	Ou' est un téléphone?	WEHT ohn teh-leh-fohn
How much does it cost?	Combien ça coûte?	com-bee-IH(n) sah coot
Where is the bathroom?	Oû sont les toilettes?	oo soh(n) leh twah-LETT
I'm sorry	Je suis désolé	zheh SWEE deh SOHLAY
excuse me, pardon me	excusez-moi pardonne moi	ex-cue-zay MWAH pahr-DOHN-eh MWAH
That's very pretty.	Ceci est très jolie.	say-see eh TRAY ZHO-lee
No, thank you.	Non, merci.	NO(n), mare-SEE
I'm very hungry.	Je suis très affamé.	zheh SWEE TRAY ah-FAH-mee
friend	ami	ah-MEE

* Chapter 5 *
Mystère à Casablanca[1]

A l'aéroport de Manaus, Brasil[2]

Thanks to the 'helpful' indigenous *Indios*, Carlos was almost ninety minutes late arriving for the next leg of his flight—to Marrakech.

"Have we missed our slot for takeoff?" Carlos asked his pilot *Jacques*.

The pilot smiled. *"Manaus n'est pas Buenos Aires, mon ami.*[3] There's not so much air traffic in and out of here that one has to worry about 'slots.' As soon as you're ready, we can leave. Do you have an appointment to meet someone in Marrakech?" *Jacques* asked. "Is there a particular time you have to be there?"

"Yes. I have to meet someone at the Marrakech airport at about 3:00 in the morning Morocco time. Let's see," Carlos was thinking, "it's almost two in the afternoon here.

---

1. Mystery in Casablanca
2. At the Airport in Manaus, Brazil
3. Manaus is not Buenos Aires, my friend.

So it must be about seven or eight in the evening there. I need to be there in eight hours, for sure. Is that a problem?"

"Not a problem at all," the pilot answered. "That is, if we get started in the next half hour."

Carlos was hungry. Hunger and fatigue were the two biggest enemies of those in his line of work. "Let's grab a good meal here in the *café*[4] before we leave, then. I need to eat," he said.

The copilot, *Georges*, spoke up. "We have excellent hot meals in the galley of the Gulfstream, sir. We thought you would want to eat. There's enough for a hot meal after we take off and another one before we land in Marrakech. You can have your choice of wild duck, poached halibut or *escargot* and *quinoa*."

"*Excellent*,"[5] Carlos said. "Then let's get going."

Carlos' gleaming Gulfstream G550 stood out like a castle among outhouses on the private plane park outside the airport terminal. In keeping with the big puma's lifestyle, it was simply the best of the best. Sleek and fast, it could fly at more than 600 miles per hour at an altitude of more than 50,000 feet. The trip to Marrakech from Manaus would take only a little more than six and a half hours.

Settled in the copilot's seat, *Georges* called the tower. "Manaus Departure, this is Gulfstream lima-victor, charlie-tango-papa ready for departure for Marrakech."

✳ ✳ ✳

---

4. coffee shop
5. "Excellent."

Pres de Marrakech au Maroc[6]

Dusty could tell Cincinnati was a little on edge. She was listening to him talking with the tower at Marrakech.

"Sabreliner niner-niner-alpha, can you go around once?" the voice from the tower asked. "We have inbound Air France from Paris on final."

"No, Marrakech. We can't go around. I'm down to less than 600 pounds of fuel. Running dry. We need to come straight in," Cincinnati responded.

"Are you declaring an emergency, Sabreliner?" the tower voice asked.

"Not yet, Marrakech. But it will be worse than an emergency if we can't come straight in," Cincinnati said with an edge in his voice.

"Very well, Sabreliner. You're cleared straight in. Emergency vehicles rolling."

"Air France heavy, we have an emergency with a private Sabreliner. Can you go around once?" the tower spoke to a commercial flight from Paris.

Cincinnati was exasperated. He turned to Dusty. "I said we didn't have an emergency, and this guy's practically calling out all the king's horses and all the king's men. Plus the French Foreign Legion. Rats! I should have put down at the Canary Islands when that tail wind didn't show up."

"Marrakech tower, this is Air France heavy. No problem. We'll go around and let the inexperienced Sabreliner have the concrete first," came the reply from the Air France inbound flight from Paris.

---

6. Near Marrakech in Morocco

"Thank you, Air France heavy," Cincinnati said. "My mistake, sir," Cincinnati spoke to the flight crew of the commercial airliner. "We'll get out of your way quickly."

Cincinnati made a sharp left turn, lowered his flaps twenty percent and pushed the nose of his little jet down. "Gear down," he said to Dusty as the Sabreliner shuddered and slowed. "And locked. I'm getting on and off this runway in a hurry. That guy's right, in a way, but he didn't have to say 'inexperienced.' I'll bet I have more hours in the air than he does."

As the little Sabreliner touched down, Dusty spoke on the intercom to Buzzer and the twins back in the cabin. "Look out the port side, sports fans," she said. "You'll see some fire trucks and an ambulance running alongside on the taxiway, lights flashing. The controller in the tower pulled the trigger on 'emergency.' But we don't have a real emergency. Just a little low on fuel, that's all."

"Wow. Look at them, Luisa," Luigi called to his little twin. "They must think we're about to blow up or come unglued."

Luisa craned her neck to see out the window.

"Maybe we should at least pretend to be hurt, or sick or something," she said. "All that action for no good reason might make somebody grouchy, don't you think?"

"Yeah. Cincinnati, for sure," Buzzer said. "And me, too. We wanted to just slip in here, nose around a little to see if we can figure out what Carlos is up to stopping here, and then be on our way. Quietly. And anonymously.

"So much for that," Buzzer concluded as Cincinnati and Dusty turned off the main runway and headed for the private plane terminal ramp.

Luigi and Luisa could see the lights of a Chevron truck heading for the same spot, most likely to fill their fuel tanks for the run into Paris.

Inside the terminal building, not much was happening. The only action was around the Air France counter where passengers for a return flight to Paris had started to line up to check in. Buzzer guessed the flight from Paris would turn around and head back in a couple of hours.

Luigi was first to see a man sleeping on a bench. What drew his attention to the sleeper were the beautiful Savile Row suit the man was wearing and the sign lying beside him that read simply 'Carlos, T.P.'

"Look Buzz," Luigi said quietly. "Do you think that guy might be waiting for the same Carlos we're after?"

Buzzer looked at the sleeping man and his sign. He turned to Dusty. "Dusty, would you take Luigi and Luisa to the *café* and get them something to eat. Go ahead and order something for Cincinnati and me, too.

"I think Cincinnati and I will have a few quiet words with that chap. I'm not sure why he would be here 24 hours early, if he's waiting for the same Carlos, but it's worth checking out."

Dusty was disappointed. Here she was baby-sitting, in effect, while Buzzer and the dancing pig did all the detective work. But the excitement of a low-fuel landing still had a hold on her. So she took Luigi and Luisa by the paws and led them toward a small *café* in the corner of the terminal.

Meanwhile, Buzzer and Cincinnati walked over to stand by the bench where the man slept. Cincinnati nudged the man's arm and shook him gently.

"*Excuse moi,*"[7] Cincinnati said. "*Reveilles-toi.*[8] We'd like to have a word with you."

"He's a sound sleeper, Cincinnati," Buzzer said when the man only grunted and kept right on sleeping.

Buzzer jumped up on the bench and walked right up to the man's face. "Hey! Wake up," he shouted.

Startled, the sleeper came to life and sat up instantly. He looked at Buzzer, then at Cincinnati. "*Que-ce-qu'ly a? Que-ce-que veus tu.*"[9] he said, shaking his head to try to get fully awake.

Cincinnati smiled and spoke softly. "My name is Cincinnati, and this is my friend Buzzer Louis. I'm a dancer, and he's a farmer. But we're much more than that. And we need to ask you a few questions."

"*Pourquoi dois je vous repondre a vos questions?*"[10] the man asked with a tense tone in his voice.

"I said we were much more than a dancer and a farmer. If you don't answer our questions," Cincinnati said softly, "then you'll find out how much more. And you don't want to do that. Does he, Buzzer?"

"I certainly wouldn't think so," Buzzer answered, winking at the dancing pig. "Remember the last guy who didn't want to answer our questions, Cincinnati?" Buzzer grinned.

"Ooo, yes I do, Buzzer. I bet he wishes he could go back and do that interview over. From the first question."

"So, my friend, what's it going to be?" Buzzer asked the man who was now wide-eyed and wide awake.

---

7. "Excuse me"
8. "Wake up, please"
9. "What is it? What do you want?"
10. "Why should I answer your questions?"

"We just have a few questions. Simple questions. And, if you cooperate we'd be pleased to buy you a cup of that thick black stuff you folks call *café*.[11] Right, Cincinnati?"

"Right you are, Buzzer." Turning to the man on the bench, Cincinnati added, "And if you don't cooperate, we'll buy you something else. Something more long lasting."

"*Bon, bon, posez moi vos questions*,"[12] he said as he started to stand up. "*Pour commencer, je m'appelle . . .*"[13]

Cincinnati interrupted him. "We don't care about your name. And don't stand up. Just sit there, please. You answer a few questions, and you'll never see or hear from us again."

"*Bien, je comprends. Continuez*,"[14] the anonymous man said, now wide-awake. And more than a little frightened of these two strange characters who had awakened him. He looked at Cincinnati and tried not to shake.

"That's better," Cincinnati said. "We mean you no harm. We're the good guys. But we're curious about the sign you have. Here's the first question: Who's this Carlos, T.P.?"

The man's eyes opened wide. He looked right and left as if to be sure nobody but Buzz and Cincinnati could hear his answer.

"I swear I don't know. I'm on a job. I'm supposed to meet someone called Carlos, T.P. here at the airport and drive him in a rented car. You can check with the Budget counter over there. He has a reservation," the man concluded.

---

11. Coffee
12. "Okay, okay. Ask me your questions."
13. "To start with, my name is . . ."
14. "Good. I understand. Go ahead."

"Where will you take him?" Buzzer asked.

"I don't know that, either. I don't know who he is or where he wants to go. His agent just told me to be here 24 hours ahead of his expected arrival in case he got here early, I guess. Seems like a waste of time to me, but they're paying me well. Very well. So here I am. Sitting here waiting."

"Or sleeping," Buzzer added. Then he turned to Cincinnati. "Why don't you keep our new friend company while I wander over to the Budget counter. Not that I think you're lying, Sir," he said to the man, "but so we won't have to bother you any further, don't you see?"

As Buzz walked up to the Budget Rent-a-Car counter, he could see a reservation folder with the name Carlos, T.P. printed boldly in black marker on the top. So far, so good. He got the attention of the lady behind the counter.

"*Comment peux je Vous aider, Monsieur.*"[15]

Buzzer answered, "I'm supposed to meet an old friend here, but I've misplaced my notes on his exact arrival time. I wonder if you have a reservation for him that might tell me if I'm early. Or late?"

"*Quel est son nom, Monsieur?*"[16] the clerk asked.

"Carlos," Buzzer answered, "Carlos, T.P."

The clerk looked at the reservations and pulled out a little folder with Carlos' name on it.

She turned to Buzzer. "Yes, sir, he does have a reservation. And it says he will arrive by private jet tomorrow night—likely about midnight."

"Just to be sure we're talking about the right Carlos,"

---

15. "How may I help you, Sir?"
16. "What's his name, Sir?"

Buzzer said, "does the reservation say where he intends to go in the rental car?"

"Yes sir, it does," she said. "Arrival after midnight in a private jet. Reserved a Mercedes stretch limousine. And will go to Casablanca and back, returning the car here by 7:00 A.M. Does that help you? He must be important. We're staying open late for him."

"That's the right guy, okay," Buzzer smiled. "*Merci, Mademoiselle, Vous nous avez bien aidé.*"[17] He added, "Looks like I'm just a day early."

Buzzer walked back to where Cincinnati and the man waiting to meet Carlos were chatting. *Seems they've struck up a friendship*, Buzzer thought.

"Are we good to go?" Cincinnati asked Buzzer.

"Yep, Cincinnati. Our nameless friend here is clean as a cat's whisker, and we owe him a cup of that thick, syrupy *café*."[18]

"Here you go, friend," Cincinnati said to the man, handing him a crisp 50 *dirham* note, the *dirham* being the currency of Morocco. "Have a late dinner or an early breakfast with our thanks."

Buzzer added, "And never tell anyone about our little meeting. Or you *will* see us again."

Luigi and Luisa, ever the adventurous eaters, were sampling a heaping helping of *couscous* in the coffee shop. Dusty, the food traditionalist, was eating scrambled eggs. When she saw Buzzer and Cincinnati walk in, she quickly swal-

---

17. "Thank you, Miss. You've been very helpful."
18. coffee

lowed the last bite of her bacon—so as not to upset Cincinnati.

The twins were into their Ma and Pa Kettle impersonations once again.

"Ma, you've done whipped up a gourmet's delight of a furin dish here. What d'ya call this stuff anyway?" Luigi said.

"I call it dee-licious, Pa, an' that's all you need to know. Just you eat it up. And let yer vittles stop yer mouth for a while," Luisa replied.

Cincinnati looked at Dusty. "I see those two are already in Paris being the Kettles, huh?" he said.

"Yes, I'm afraid so," Dusty said. "They're certainly entertaining themselves, but they're about to drive me bonkers. I hope they don't plan to be Ma and Pa the whole time we're in Paris. That could be a nightmare."

Luigi was listening. He looked at Dusty and decided to go ahead and say what he thought needed to be said.

"Dusty," he began, "in Paris we'll be working. The two of us may just come up with another stupendous plan to capture Carlos, like we did a few days ago in Buenos Aires. There won't be much time for Ma and Pa games, if you know what I mean. And I think you do.

"So why don't you give us the benefit of the doubt for a change? We know the difference between work and play."

Luigi looked to Luisa for reaction. She gave him a secret low four under the table and smiled sweetly at Dusty.

Buzzer changed the subject. "We know we're almost a full day ahead of Carlos right now. And we know he's going to spend three or four hours driving to Casablanca and back once he gets here. He can't possibly be in Paris before mid-morning tomorrow—30 hours from now. So we'll have time to get settled in and be ready for him."

"Yes, but what we don't know is why he's taking this little side trip to Casablanca," Cincinnati said. "Maybe we better get to your cousin *René* as soon as we get to Paris and ask him to alert Interpol and the local authorities in Casablanca. Just to be on the safe side."

Dusty, who was almost over her chastisement by Luigi, interrupted the conversation. "I suggest Buzzer and Cincinnati eat their food and then we get on our way to Paris. I need to get there and get some rest. Or get some rest here and go to Paris in the morning."

"We go on tonight," Buzzer said. "*dans un demi heure.*" [19]

What do you think Carlos is planning to do in Casablanca? Why isn't he just flying there directly? Why rent a car, or limousine, and drive there and back? Or has he just made up a wild story for the people at Budget Rent-a-Car? Will Luigi and Luisa keep playing Ma and Pa Kettle? Or will Dusty make them stop?

---

19. "In half an hour."

Parlez Vous Francais?

by Cincinnati

Now we're going to learn about weather. *C'est important de comprendre paroles et frases significatif.*[20]

English	French	Say It Like This
weather	*temps*	TOMP
climate	climat	KLIMA
It's hot.	Il fait chaud.	eel feh SHAWD
It's cold.	C'est froid.	sest FRAHD
It's windy.	Il y a du vent.	eel ee ah duh vahnt
rain	pluie	PLUI
It's raining.	Il pleut.	eel PLEU
snow	neige	NEZH
cloud	nuage	noo-AZH
storm	tempête	TÃPET
thunder	tonnerre	tohn-EHR
lightning	éclair	EK-lehr
hail	grêle	GREHL
temperature	temperature	TÃ-pehr-ah-tyoor
sun	soleil	so-lizh
sunlight	luminère	luhm-eh-NYEHR
moon	lune	loon
moonlight	clair de lune	KLER deh loon

---

20. It's important to understand significant words and phrases about the weather.

Part Two

How You Gonna Keep 'Em Down on the Ranch?

"Paris is my town. From *Rive Gauche* to *Montmartre*, I know every inch of it. Just call it 'Cincinnati on the *Seine*.' Carlos will never be able to hide from me. I guarantee it . . . on my mammy's hammy."

—Cincinnati
Pilot, detective and
dancer

* Chapter 6 *

Un jour de fête pour les detectives dans la ville de lumière[1]

La Brigade Criminelle—Au travail[2]

"*Le Bourget* Tower, this is Sabreliner seven-zero-niner-niner-alpha, fifty-five miles southwest requesting landing instructions." Dusty spoke to the traffic controllers at a small, out-of-the-way airport north of Paris after a long day and night of flying.

It was five o'clock in the morning as *The Flying Pig Machine* touched down after a pass over Paris. The city was lit up like a Christmas tree, street lamps and neon signs blazing into the black night sky.

Luigi and Luisa had time on the flight from Marrakech to watch *Ma and Pa Kettle* for the third time in 24 hours. Not only had they perfected their impersonations, but also

---

1. A Holiday for Detectives in the City of Light
2. Criminal Brigade—On the job

they had finished the list of sights they wanted to see in the city.

Buzzer had hinted that since they were so far ahead of Carlos, there might be some time the first day to do a little sightseeing. After everyone had slept, of course. And after they had met with Buzzer's cousin *René Francois Fopaux*, newly appointed head of the *Criminelle Brigade*, and his dimwitted assistant, *Guy G. Gondeaux*. They needed *René's* help to officially alert the authorities in Marrakech and Casablanca that an infamous international terrorist might be heading their way.

René had arranged for a private hangar for *The Flying Pig Machine*—a place where they could hide the plane from Carlos and his agents, and maybe keep the big puma from finding out they, too, were in Paris.

René and *Guy* were waiting for them in the dimly lit hangar as Cincinnati rolled the little Sabreliner slowly through the big double doors. They had a French customs agent with them, an agent who insisted that all the travelers come out of the plane one at a time so he could ask his questions and stamp their passports. Individually.

"*Vous déranger la Justice international, mon petit pompeux gendarme,*"[3] *René* barked at the agent. "One more of your ridiculous little demands and I will have your nose mounted on mahogany and hung in the *Louvre* for all to see."

Guy gave a little horse-whinny laugh, and *René* glared at him menacingly. *Guy* immediately put his hands in his front

---

3. "You are messing with international justice, my pompous little martinet."

pockets and turned toward where the big double doors were sliding shut.

Luigi and Luisa noticed the customs agent had an extra large nose. "He must be the son of *Charles de Gaulle*," Luigi whispered to his sister.

"Or maybe Cyrano, Luigi," Luisa whispered back. That's quite a snozzola he's got there. It's going to take a pretty big slab of mahogany to make a plaque for it."

The twins went on with their nose jokes privately while they waited in line for their turn to be "processed" by the customs agent.

Luigi offered, "If Mr. Nose there gets a cold, he'll need a beach towel for a handkerchief."

Not to be outdone, Luisa whispered, "I think his profile may be almost as wide as it is tall. If he went snorkeling, he could use two soda cans for nose plugs."

Giggling, Luigi added, "If his face was on Mount Rushmore, the whole mountain would topple into Nebraska, and roll over and over all the way to Mexico."

Dusty noticed the tiny twins doing their best not to laugh out loud.

"Luigi," she said, "what are you laughing about? I thought you said the two of you know the difference between work and play. We're here in Paris to work."

Before Luigi could answer, Dusty found herself next in line to be questioned by the agent with the big nose.

Luisa whispered to Luigi, "His nose is so big we could both drown in one of his boogers."

That did it. The two of them fell out laughing. They sat down at the top of the stairs to The Flying Pig Machine and

laughed until they cried. And boogers came out their own little noses. That only made them laugh all the harder. Now they couldn't even look at one another without both bursting into hilarious laughter.

The best part of the fun was that Dusty was occupied with the customs agent's questioning and couldn't see what the twins were up to.

Dusty, her questioning over and her passport stamped, stepped out into the hangar and glared at the twins.

It was Luigi's turn to be "processed."

The agent looked at Luigi's passport. He said, "I see you are from *les Etats Unis—au Texas*,"[4] he said to Luigi. "*C'est exact, Monsieur?*"[5]

Luigi rolled his eyes and tilted his head this way and that. It was a sure sign to Luisa that her little twin was about to go into one of his acts.

Luigi fixed a stare on the agent and answered with a straight face, "Sir," he said, "who NOSE? My big brother NOSE where I'm from, but I'm just a little kitten. Did you ask him? I'm sure he NOSE."

Luisa went into hysterics. This was Luigi at his best. Standing up to silly authority, and having fun doing it.

"Is she your twin?" The agent pointed to Luisa, who still had tears streaming down her face as she squirmed on the little plane's pull-down staircase.

"She NOSE who she is," Luigi answered. "Why don't you ask her? Sometimes I think we're twins. But other times . . . who NOSE?"

---

4. the United States—in Texas
5. "Is that correct, Sir?"

Luigi finally lost it. He went into gales of laughter, and Luisa became hysterical once again.

The agent summoned Buzzer. "Can you answer my questions for these two little ones, sir? They seem to be having some kind of private joke going on here."

Buzzer looked at the twins, then turned to the agent. "What seems to be the problem?" he asked.

"Who *knows*, sir?" the agent replied. "I can't seem to get him to tell me what he obviously *knows*. And who *knows* what she will say when, or if, I finally get to her. I hope she *knows* more than he *knows*. But he said his big brother *knows*. And that would be you, sir."

Well, with all the "KNOWS" in the air, Luigi and Luisa were hysterical. They lay down on the stairs, put their heads on the steps and pounded those steps with all four front paws, laughing uncontrollably.

"Give me your passports," Buzzer said to the twins. He had figured out the joke, and so had Cincinnati, Dusty and *René*. Only *Guy* and the customs agent seemed not to "get it."

René turned to Dusty and asked, "Are those two always so clever?"

Even straight-laced Dusty couldn't resist. "Heaven only NOSE," she said. And Cincinnati and *René* burst into laughter, too.

Guy saw everyone else laughing and, even though he didn't have a clue why, he started laughing, too, but not before everyone else was about finished.

Cincinnati answered *René*'s question. "You can stake your life on their cleverness, *René*. They are smart, first-rate detectives. They're clever far beyond their years. We can count on them to think and act intelligently, always. And to give us all a laugh when things get thick, and we need a little tension relief."

✱ ✱ ✱

A l'aéroport Marrakech. Le jour suivant[6]

"The two of you catch a little shuteye if you want to. I'll be gone for a few hours, but I'll be back here by 7:00 A.M.," Carlos said to his pilots *Jacques* and *Georges* as they left his parked Gulfstream on the tarmac outside the Marrakech terminal.

"Let's shoot for lifting off for Paris about 7:30 so we can be there by mid-morning. And thanks to both of you for helping me brush up on my French pronunciation on the way over."

Carlos walked into the terminal and looked around. It was still quiet this early in the morning. British Air and Ryan Air flights would be leaving for London and Amsterdam, one plane after the other in a few hours. And Air France had two flights to Paris before noon.

Carlos, of course, was looking for the man who was to meet him and drive him to Casablanca, where he had work to do. He saw the sign and headed for the nicely dressed agent who held it.

---

6. Marrakech Airport. The Next Morning

"Je suis Carlos, T.P.,"[7] he said. "And before you answer, I don't want to know who you are."

"Very well, sir," the driver said. "Your Mercedes limousine is waiting, and I am prepared to take you wherever you want to go."

"Slight change of plans," Carlos announced. "We'll take a Fiat van instead of the limousine. You go to the Budget counter and make the change. Here are 500 *dirhams*. Keep whatever's left over for yourself. I'll wait by the curb out there. Pick me up as soon as you can."

As the driver took the money and headed for the Budget Rent-a-Car counter where a young woman agent looked to be sleeping, Carlos strolled out the terminal's main doors and sat down on a bench in the semi-darkness—a bench near the curb.

The big puma thought, *Five million Euros for the work of the next few days. That's more than $7 million U.S. and almost 28 million Argentinean pesos. That Ramos was a bargain. His idea of big money is chump-change. I would gladly have paid him four or five million pesos, and the poor wretch could have retired to a life of leisure. Oh, well,* he continued thinking. *That's why I'm Carlos the puma and he's Capitán Ramos, the simple master of a small boat in a small business that will never get bigger. And why I would never hire him to work with me.*

Carlos closed his eyes and began to visualize what he would do in Casablanca. It was so simple, yet so few could do it. Fewer still would be willing to.

A plain white Fiat van pulled to the curb. The well-

---

7. "I'm Carlos, T.P."

dressed driver got out, walked around to the curb and opened the back door.

Carlos stepped over to the van and closed the door. "*Je vais m'assoir devant avec vous,*"[8] he said in perfect French. "Let's go to Casablanca. To the barracks of the Foreign Legion."

* * *

Dans une Suite a l' Hôtel Georges Cinq—Paris[9]

The travelers were all very tired. They'd been in the air almost sixteen hours since leaving Buenos Aires. If it hadn't been for the twin's little "nose" game at the airport, they might have been cranky. After all, they had crossed many a border since they left their little ranch in the Hill Country of Texas seven days ago, and they had never seen such a rigmarole as the French customs agent put them through.

Once all the travelers had been cleared, processed and stamped into France, *René* had surprised the agent by placing him under "protective custody" and having *Guy Gondeaux* take him straight to a cell at the headquarters of the *Criminelle Brigade.*

René had said to the group, "We just can't take the chance that *Monsieur Bignose*[10] might talk. He knows you're in Paris. We'll hold him only a few days until this business with Carlos is settled, and then we'll release him with our profound apologies. '*Ah, un tel erreur,*'[11] I'll explain to him.

---

8. "I'll ride in front with you."
9. In a Suite in the Hotel Georges V—Paris
10. Mister Big Nose
11. 'Ah, such a mistake'

And then I'll blame it all on that imbecile Guy. Guy will never figure it out. That's what I've found him really good at—taking the fall, and never worrying about anything." *René* gave a little laugh.

"We'll register you as 'Sir Clive Ashby and party' at the *Georges Cinq*. No one but I will know you're really here in France. *Guy* knows nothing, as usual."

And they had registered with fake British passports *René* provided. Buzzer, of course, was Sir Clive, M.P. Cincinnati's cover name was Reginald Anthony, Esquire, a barrister from London. Dusty became Duchess Fiona Welch. And the twins' passports named them Nick and Nikki Andrews, exchange students, and twins, of course, from Oxford.

The twins could hardly keep their eyes open. They were tired from traveling, but also from laughing. Still, they wanted to go out and see Paris.

"When can we go to the top of the *Eiffel Tower*?" Luisa asked Buzzer. And she then asked the same question again and again—five times. Luigi counted.

"How can I get into the sewers?" Luigi asked *René*.

Finally Cincinnati, who was probably the tiredest of anybody, said to Luigi and Luisa, "*René* is going to call the authorities in Marrakech and Casablanca to alert them that Carlos may be on the way. Dusty is going to order you two *glaces a la vanille et gatêaux au chocolat*[12] from Room Service. And then we are all going to sleep for three or four hours."

Buzzer quickly added, "Then, Nick and Nikki, we'll spend the afternoon looking around. How's that?"

---

12. vanilla ice cream and chocolate cake

Well, Pa," Luisa said, "That's better'n finding there's no Sears and Roebuck catalog in the outhouse, I guess."

"Luigi went into another laughing fit, and, of course, Luisa quickly joined him.

René was finishing up his second call, the one to Casablanca. "That's right, Omar, Carlos will likely be in a Mercedes stretch limo from Budget Rent-a-Car in Marrakech. And he'll be in a hurry. Seems he's making a quick run into and out of Casablanca, and we don't know why."

He listened for a moment and added, "Okay, if you don't see him in Marrakech—and he's a master of disguise, remember—keep an eye out in Casablanca. And call me at once if he shows up. Thanks, Omar. I owe you one, at least."

As *René* turned to leave the suite and the hotel, Dusty dialed Room Service on the house phone. When they answered, she looked across the room and said, *"Peu emporte, desolée, je vais appeler plus tard à nouveau."*[13]

Luigi and Luisa, aka Nick and Nikki, had fallen sound asleep on the sofa.

What do you think Carlos will do in Casablanca? And what will he do in Paris to earn so much money? Why do you suppose he changed from a Mercedes limousine to a simple Fiat van? And what of the four Texas Cats and the dancing pig? Will the slow-witted Guy Gondeaux ever get a clue? Will Luisa get to go to the Eiffel Tower? Will Luigi see rats in the sewers? If he does, will he be scared?

---

13. "Never mind. Sorry. I'll call back later."

Parlez Vous Francais?
by Cincinnati

Now you know many French words about the weather. *Apprennons encore quelques môts, cette fois-ci au sujet de nourriture*[14]

English	French	Say It Like This
bread	pain	PAH(n)
butter	buerre	BURR
milk	lait	LAY
toast	pain grillé	PAH(n) gree-YEH
bacon	bacon, Lard	BEK-un, LAH
ham	jambon	zhahm-BOH(n)
waffle	gaufre	gauf-FREH
cream	crème	CRIM
cheese	fromage	froh-MAHZH
beef	boeuf	BUFF
fish	poisson	pwah-SOH(n)
chicken	poulet	poo-LAY
soup	potage	poh-TAZH
salad	salade	sah-LAHD
potato	pomme	POHM
rice	riz	REE
vegetables	légumes	leh-GUHM
fruits	rruits	fruh-EE
water	eau	OH
salt	sel	SELL
pepper	poivre	PWAH-vrah
sugar	sucre	SEU-cruh

---

14. Let's learn some more words, this time about food.

* Un jour de fête pour les detectives dans la ville de lumière *

eggs	oeuf	UFF
candy	sucre candi, bonbon	SEU-cruh, cahn-DEE, bohn-BOHN
chocolate	chocolat	shoh-coh-LAH
beans	haricots	ah-ree-COH
tomato	tomate	Toh-MAHT
grapes	raisin	RAY-szeh(n)

* Chapter 7 *

Le sommet de la Tour, les rats de l'égout et casernes en feu[1]

Curiosité a Casablanca[2]

It was 5:00 A.M. in Casablanca. "Step on it, please," Carlos said to the anonymous driver of the Fiat van. "I need to be back at the airport in Marrakech 7:00."

The driver pushed the accelerator harder, and the speedometer crept up to 140 kilometers per hour—almost 90 miles per hour. There was little traffic so early in the morning, and Carlos knew the almost-new van was capable of going pretty fast, at least for a couple of hours.

The driver looked far down the road trying to see beyond the headlight beams' reach. "You weren't in there more than five minutes, sir. It's a long round trip to Casablanca for a five minute meeting," he said.

"There was no meeting," the big puma responded. "I

---

1. Tower Tops, Sewer Rats and Barracks Burning
2. Curiosity in Casablanca

just had to pick up some things near the fence behind the barracks and then deliver them to the front door. That's all."

"I'm happy to have the job of driving you," the driver said, "but I could've made the run for you. Even yesterday. Saved you the trouble."

"My friend," Carlos replied, "there may be no more than three or four others in the world who could have—or would have—done what I just did. No more questions. Let's just say you will know about what I've done before the day is out. It was a favor for a French client. And now I must go to Paris to finish the job for him."

Dans la suite de l'hôtel Georges Cinq [3]

Luisa was the first to wake up from her nap. She was surprised to think she had slept more than four hours. It was almost 11:00 A.M.

Seeing everybody else was still sleeping, the little kitten grabbed up the house phone and called *le service de chambre*.[4] Speaking in a high-pitched nasal tone to disguise her voice when the kitchen answered, she said, "This is the Duchess Fiona Welch in room 435. We require two extra large slices of chocolate cake, lots of icing please, and two bowls of two scoops each of vanilla ice cream, and with chocolate sauce

---

3. In the suite at the *Georges Cinq Hotel*—George V Hotel.
4. Room Service

on top. As quickly as possible. Of course, they're for my twin niece and nephew, Nick and Nikki. They're growing, and they're simply ravenous little beasts."

She listened for a moment, then added, "Thank you ever so much. Charge it to Sir Clive's room. He's a Member of Parliament, you know. And add five Euros for the person who delivers it. Assuming they are prompt, to be sure."

When she put the phone down, Luigi was sitting up, watching her and grinning. He said, as Pa Kettle, "Where'd ya learn to speak so haughty-like Ma? You sound like you's a hoity-toity English lady, or maybe a movie star."

"Just you never mind, Pa," she said. "It gits the job done, don't it? The best lunch you ever had's on the way, an' if you don't flap yer jaws too much and make too much noise, we might be able to eat it and hide the evidence before the evil queen in there," she pointed to Dusty's room, "wakes up and puts a spell on us."

Just then Dusty Louise poked her head out her door. "Did you order some cake and ice cream for the evil queen, too?" she asked.

Caught in the middle of what might turn unpleasant, Luigi grabbed the phone and punched up Room Service.

"Ah, right-o," he said. "This is Sir Clive, M.P., in room 435. I'm told on excellent authority—excellent, indeed— that Duchess Fiona has ordered two servings of cake and ice cream for our niece and nephew. 'Well,' I said to her, 'that was a jolly good cock-up. What about the rest of us, Fiona?' So we've all decided we should relish chocolate cake and ice cream as well. Please, if you will, increase that order to five servings and oh yes, increase the gratuity to ten Euros.

He listened, "Yes, we shall all be grateful to you, Room Service, whoever you are. We look forward to having our appetites sated by some lovely *Patisserie française et glaces.*[5] And do rush it up, if you please. Our anticipation is devilishly debilitating, you see. And, just between us, the Duchess Fiona turns into the wicked queen when she's made to wait too long."

Luigi had disarmed Dusty. Much as she wanted to correct the twins for their mischief, she had to laugh at their latest antics. *They've been cooped up too long, she thought. We need to get them a good sugar high with cake and ice cream and then get them out of this room and this hotel onto the streets of Paris where they can burn off some of their pent-up energy.*

Retour a l'aeroport de Marrakech[6]

Carlos thanked the anonymous driver and tipped him an additional 500 dirhams. "You will forget this job, immediately," Carlos said to him sternly. "You have never met or heard of Carlos, T.P. And you most certainly did not go to Casablanca, today or in the last month, or the next month. Is that clear?"

"As you say, whoever you may be whom I've never heard of or seen before," the driver smiled. He slipped the extra *dirhams* into his pocket, turned and disappeared into a crowd coming off a redeye British Airways flight from London.

Carlos looked at the clock on the wall behind the Air France counter. It was 7:20 in the morning. It would be

---

5. French pastries and ice cream
6. Back at the Airport in Marrakech

forty minutes before the "gift" he had left at the Foreign Legion barracks in Casablanca was discovered.

And what a discovery that would be.

He headed for the private pilot's lounge to collect *Jacques* and *Georges*. Carlos wanted to be in the air on the way to Paris at 8:00 A.M.

The perfect alibi.

✳ ✳ ✳

Les rues de Paris[7]

Cincinnati, Dusty and the twins stood on the sidewalk outside the American Express office on *Rue Scribe* while Buzzer went inside to collect the 5,000 Euros Socks had wired to them for incidental expenses.

Wired, themselves, with a sugar high from the generous helpings of vanilla ice cream and chocolate cake (with plenty of icing), Luigi and Luisa were fidgeting, anxious to get going to work their way through their list of sights to see in Paris.

As Buzzer came out the door tucking crisp bills into his fanny pack, Luigi spoke up. "Now can we go to the sewers?" he asked, adding, "I want to see some of those rats and smell the smells that make this place so famous!"

Luisa countered, "First, let's go to the top of the *Eiffel Tower*. That way we can see the whole city at once and then decide what else we want to see next."

Buzzer, ever the peace maker, looked at the twins and said, "I want to see the *Seine et la rive gauche*[8] first. Then

---

7. The Streets of Paris
8. The Seine is a river that winds through Paris. The left bank is one side of it, *rive gauche* in French.

we'll go up the tower and down into the sewers. In fact," he added, "I just arranged a four-hour tour in the American Express office that will take us to all three places, plus a couple more on your list, guys. It's best to get an overview—in the air from the *Eiffel Tower* and on the streets—before we start going to specific places. A small bus will pick us up here in about fifteen minutes. Luisa, we'll go to the top of the *Eiffel Tower* and Luigi, we'll get a good look down in the sewers. Plus a whole lot more, all this afternoon."

Luisa, ever the *provocateur*,[9] whispered to Luigi, "There really are rats in the sewers, you know. Millions of them. And some of them are as big as muskrats."

Luigi caught his breath, eyes wide, and he said, "We don't have to talk to them, do we? Or even get very close?"

Luisa laughed. "You're the one who wants to go into the sewers so badly, Luigi. I just hope those huge rats don't work for Carlos or decide to attack us."

"What's the matter, Luigi?" Dusty said. "You don't look so well." She noticed the little kitten was agitated and pale. He was breathing fast.

"I'm okay, Dusty," he answered. "It's probably just a little too much ice cream."

Le matin suivant, sur Casablanca dans l'avion de Carlos[10]

Carlos' G550 left Marrakech at 7:30 in the morning, just as the big cat had wanted. A half hour later, as they

---

9. "Provocateur" is a French word often used in speaking English. It means someone who starts trouble or issues challenges.
10. The Next Morning, Over Casablanca in Carlos' Plane

passed over Casablanca, *Jacques* flipped on the intercom and spoke to Carlos in the cabin.

"*Regarde la' bas c'est Casablanca,*"[11] he said. "There's a huge fireball on the west side of the city. Flames are shooting way up into the air. What do you suppose that's all about, Boss?" Carlos didn't answer. He didn't look out the window, either. He knew precisely *what that was all about."*

The big cat just smiled and settled back in his plush leather recliner where he would sleep for the next two hours until they landed at *Charles de Gaulle* International Airport in Paris.

He thought, *What that was all about was part one of my next job – the first step to another five million Euros for me, Carlos the puma. In a few days I'll finish this job, send my pay to Switzerland and the Cayman Islands, and then go after that tuxedo cat and his pig friend. Those dratted little kittens, too. They will pay for crossing Carlos. They will pay.*

He closed his eyes and immediately went to sleep.

Why do you suppose Carlos bombed the French Foreign Legion barracks in Casablanca? If that was the first part of his new job to earn five million Euros, what do you suppose he's going to do in Paris? Will Luisa get to go to the top of the Eiffel *Tower? And what about Luigi? Are there really millions of rats in the sewers of Paris? Do some of them work for Carlos, do you think? Are they really as big as muskrats? Will they attack Luigi and Luisa?*

---

11. "Look to the left at Casablanca."

Parlez Vous Francais?

by Cincinnati

Now that you know how to say at least some of your favorite foods in French, *apprennons de plus sur les jours, le semaines, les mois et le calendrier.*[12]

English	French	Say It Like This
today	*aujourd'hui*	oh-zhohr-DWEE
yesterday	*hier*	ee-AIR
day before yesterday	*avant-hier*	ah-vahn tee-AIR
tomorrow	*demain*	deh-MAHN
day after tomorrow	*après-demain*	ah-PRAY deh-MAHN
this week	*cette semaine*	set teh-MEHN
last week	*la semaine derniere*	lah seh-mehn– deh-NYAIR
next week	*la semaine prochaine*	lah seh-mehn proh-SHEN
week before last	*la semaine avant la derniere*	lah seh-mehn ah-vahn la deh-NYAIR
week after next	*la semaine après la prochaine*	la seh-mehn ah-PREH lah proh-SHIN
this month	*ce mois ci*	say MWAH see
last month	*le mois dernier*	le MWAH dehr-NYAIR
next month	*le mois prochain*	le MWAH deu pro-SHAH(n)
eight A.M.	*huit heure du matin*	WEET uhr deu mah-TAHT(n)
noon	*midi*	mee-DEE
six P.M.	*six heure de l'après-midi*	see ehrh de la-preh-mee-DEE
midnight	*minuit*	meen-WEE

---

12. Let's learn more about days, weeks, months and the calendar.

* Chapter 8 *
Pour attraper un chat[1]

Aujourd'hui un representant de diamant sud african[2]

Carlos gently placed a small black case he had brought with him from his green shack in the rain forest into the boot of a long black Mercedes limousine at the curb outside the private plane terminal at *Charles de Gaulle* International Airport near Paris. He climbed into the front seat beside his *chauffeur*.[3]

Jacques and *Georges*, Carlos' pilot and co-pilot, had stayed behind to arrange a hanger space for the big cat's sleek G550. They would join him at the hotel later in the day.

"*Conduize-moi a l'hôtel Ritz de Paris*,"[4]

---

1. To Catch a Cat
2. Today a South African Diamond Salesman
3. Driver. A French word often used in English.
4. Take me to the Paris Ritz

Carlos said to his *chauffeur*. "Today I'm a diamond salesman from South Africa. They know me only as a diamond salesman there. Then go on back to the airport to pick up *Jacques* and *Georges, s'il vous plait.*"[5]

Carlos leaned back in the plush seat, closed his eyes and immediately fell to sleep, completely unaware of the traffic and commotion outside the limo.

Les roues de Paris[6]

A twelve-passenger Peugeot van pulled smartly to the curb outside the American Express office.

"Here's our tour bus," Buzzer announced. The four cats and the dancing pig climbed up the steps through the front door and took seats among a German couple from Hamburg and a Canadian Mountie and his young daughter on vacation from Montreal.

The van's driver flipped a switch on the microphone sticking out of the dashboard in front of him and said, "*Bienvenues au Tours de Paris. Mon nom est Philip. Nous pouvons parler Anglais, Français et Allemand aujourd'hui. Quel est votre choix?*"[7]

Luisa couldn't resist. She leaned over to Dusty and said in an exaggerated voice, "I think we can all understand French, don't you, *ma soeur?*[8]

Dusty was not pleased. She called out to the driver, "If it's okay with the rest of the passengers, we would like to speak English, please."

---

5. if you please
6. The Streets of Paris
7. "Welcome to Tours of Paris. My name is Philip. We can speak English, French or German today. What is your pleasure?"
8. my sister

"Very well, Madam," the driver replied. "Our first stop will be the left bank of the Seine. And then we'll go to the famous *Eiffel Tower* so you can see the rooftops of Paris. We'll finish our little tour at the equally famous Paris sewers, where you will meet some very interesting local rats, I'm sure.

"Sit back, relax and, please, ask questions of me whenever you think of one. And enjoy the sights, sounds and smells of the greatest city in the world."

Immediately Luigi blurted out his first question: "Are we there yet?"

Luisa burst out laughing.

Buzzer and Cincinnati smiled, but Dusty was not amused.

As the tour van pulled into heavy traffic, a light rain began to fall. The tour guide, spoke into his microphone. "*Madames et Monsieurs, chats et cochon, il pleut ouvent Paris.*[9] A little rain will not spoil our afternoon. I have several *parapluies*[10] here, and you are welcome to use them at any of our stops along the way."

* * *

Paris Hôtel Ritz a la Réception[11]

Le réceptionist[12] greeted Carlos in the customary snooty manner of hotels such as the Ritz. "Ah, Mr. Diamond Salesman. Welcome again to the Paris Ritz. We have re-

---

9. "Ladies and gentlemen, cats and pig, it rains often in Paris."
10. umbrellas
11. Paris Ritz Hotel Reception Desk
12. desk clerk

served for you your usual luxury suite, sir. And we're so glad to see you once more."

"Good morning to you as well, Pierre," Carlos answered. "I need to ask a couple of favors. First, this black bag contains my diamond samples worth many millions of Euros; can you put it into the hotel safe, and will I be able to retrieve it any time of the day or night?"

"*Mais, certainment, Monsieur.*"[13] It will be safely kept, and if you will call the desk a few minutes before you need it, the case will be waiting for you right here. What else can I do for you?" Pierre asked.

"I left home in a bit of a rush yesterday, Pierre, and neglected to change my money. Can you change 100,000 Argentine pesos to Euros for me, *s'il te plait?*"[14]

"Ah, most certainly, sir. We don't keep that kind of money at hand, but I'll send one of my assistants to the bank immediately, and your Euros will be ready momentarily. That should be about 22,000 Euros, more or less. Shall I send them up to your suite?"

"*Non, merci, Pierre.*[15] Please just put them in the safe with my sample case. I'm very tired now, and I need to take a nap, for sure."

"Anything else, *Monsieur?*" Pierre asked.

"Just one more thing. I will be expecting many guests during my stay. None must come to my suite unless I'm notified first. Some will be very important clients, and some may appear—how shall I say?—a bit unsavory. Gypsies, to

---

13. "But, of course, Sir."
14. please
15. "No, thank you, Pierre."

be exact. However, they, too, are very important to my business. Perhaps you will escort them up on the service elevator? I'll meet with the more respectable looking clients in the famous Hemingway Bar.

"But I don't want to be seen in public with the Gypsies, no? And you certainly don't want them in any of your bars," Carlos said.

"Most thoughtful of you, *Monsieur*," Pierre said. "We both have our reputations to consider. You may be sure of the utmost discretion here at the Ritz."

"Exactly why I choose to stay here, Pierre," Carlos smiled. "Now I must get to my room and get some sleep."

As he accompanied a bellman to the elevators, Carlos knew fresh flowers and an assortment of delicate pastries and coffee were already on their way. They would be there waiting for him as if that's where they were always kept for the diamond salesman, a most favored guest.

A la Tour Eiffel[16]

Philip began to speak as the tour van pulled into the circular drive in front of the *Eiffel Tower*.

"Here we are at what is perhaps the most famous, and certainly the most recognizable, structure in the world—the famous *Eiffel Tower*. Designed by 19th century Parisian architect Gustave Eiffel for the Exposition of 1889, it is made entirely of iron members held together by more than 2,500,000 rivets.

"The entire tower is repainted every seven years. Each

---

16. At the *Eiffel Tower*

coat requires 50,000 gallons of paint.

"You may go to the top on elevators and see the entire city and far beyond. If you are adventurous enough to wish to climb the stairs, you can also do that. But not today, I'm afraid. We only have forty-five minutes on our schedule here, and that's not nearly enough time for a climb. Enjoy your visit, and meet me right back here in exactly 45 minutes.

"Please don't be late. We still have the sewers to visit.

"Oh, and one more thing. Be cautious of anyone approaching you to sell you souvenirs of any kind. Avoid anyone who asks you for money. These people prey on unsuspecting visitors. Let me just say that many of them are not exactly honest. See you in three-quarters of an hour."

"I want an *Eiffel Tower* pencil sharpener," Luigi said to Luisa as they scrambled off the bus and headed for the elevators.

"That's ridiculous, Luigi. Whatever would you do with such a thing?"

"Sharpen pencils. What else?" Luigi retorted.

"Get on that elevator, you two!" Dusty Louise was into her kitten-herding mode, and she was already worried about getting back to the tour van in 43 more minutes.

On the top deck, looking out over the city of Paris, Luisa couldn't resist another Ma and Pa Kettle conversation. "Just you lookee yonder, Pa," she said to Luigi. "I reckon we's higher'n the Umpire State Building up here. Them people down there look like ants, don't they?"

"Shurr nuff they do, Ma," Luigi answered, "and the cars and buildins look like toys. Why, I could sharpen a pencil big as a train if this was a pencil sharpener instead o' just a tower. It don't do nothin'. Just stands here lookin' important."

Even as Pa Kettle, Luigi was into changing subjects with his own brand of jump-speak.

"Reckon I could jump offa here if'n I had a parachute, Pa?" Luisa asked Luigi.

"Betcha could, Ma, but if the wind was blowin' strong, you might end up in Spain. Or Elbow Macaronia."

Cincinnati was listening, amused. "I think you mean Albania, Pa Kettle," he said.

"No, he means Elbow Macaronia, Cincinnati," Luisa answered. "It's where he says he's going to teach English and write his book about strange things . . . after he graduates from Sister Mary Cannonball's kindergarten. Right, Luigi?"

"I could do that, yes," he said. "But I might become a world-famous actor, instead. Or a bullfighter. Or even a senator. Who NOSE?"

With the nose reference, the two kittens began laughing hilariously once again.

Dusty, watching the time and still having problems with Luigi and Luisa amusing themselves, announced, "Time to go. We don't want to miss the rest of the tour."

"And those rats in the sewer," Buzzer added, turning to Luigi. "You do want to see the rats, don't you, Luigi?"

Luisa chimed in, "Even the ones as big as muskrats?"

Luigi smiled. "You think I'm afraid of a few big rats, don't you? If they get me, they're going to get you, too. Let's go."

✳ ✳ ✳

Dans la Suite de Carlos a l'Hôtel Ritz[17]

Carlos had been asleep less than two hours when the phone in his suite rang. And kept ringing until he decided he had no choice but to answer it.

"*Allo,*"[18] he said, wishing he could sleep another hour or two.

"Mr. Diamond Salesman, this is Pierre downstairs. I'm so sorry to disturb you. But there have been numerous calls for you in the past half hour, all from the same gentleman with an Eastern European accent. He has become very insistent. He claims he's a count who has urgent business with you. Do you wish to speak with him, sir? Or what shall we tell him?"

"Thank you, Pierre. He is, in fact, a count. And I do need to speak with him. Ask him to call back in ten minutes. I'll have another cup of this coffee and try to get awake."

"Very well, *Monsieur,*" Pierre said, disconnecting the call.

Carlos thought the call could have waited a few hours,

---

17. In Carlos' Suite at the Ritz Hotel
18. "Hello"

but this caller—the count—was, after all, putting up 5,000,000 Euros for the job the big puma would finish for him here in Paris. *Better I take the call now than risk that much money. I can sleep afterward after I explain how I intend to do what he is paying me to do.*

Carlos pumped himself a fresh cup of hot, black coffee from the silver hotpot, put two pastries and a napkin on a small china plate, and sat down by the telephone.

He was now wide awake.

Who do you think is calling Carlos? What is the job Carlos the puma has to finish for him? Will Luigi really go into the sewers? If he does, will he see millions of rats? Will some of them be as big as muskrats? And what are René Francois Fopaux *and* Guy Gondeaux *up to while Cincinnati and the Texas cats are looking over the sights of Paris?*

Parlez Vous Francais?
by Cincinnati

Now you know more about the calendar and dates, *Apprennons quelque chose au sujet vetêments.*[19] What would you wear if it were raining in Paris as it is today? What if it were very cold? Or really hot?

English	French	Say It Like This
hat	chapeau	shah-POH
shirt	chemise	sheh-MEEZ
blouse	blouse, chemisette	BLUEZ, sheh-mee-ZHET
pants	pantalon	pahn-tah-LOH(n)
skirt	jupe	ZHEUP
dress	robe	ROHB
shoes	chaussures	shah-SZEUR
socks	chausettes	shah-SET
belt	cinture	SAHN-teur
coat	manteau	mahn-TEAU
jacket	veste	VEST
boots	bottes	BOHT
scarf	écharpe	eh SHARP
gloves	gants	GAH(n)
raincoat	imperméable	ahm-PAIR-meh-ah-bluh
umbrella	parapluie	pahr-ah-PLUEE
underwear	souvêtement	soo-vet-MAH(n)

---

19. Let's learn something about clothing.

* Chapter 9 *
Comptes, Chats, Cochons, Rats[1]

Les égouts de Paris[2]

Philip the tour guide pulled the van to a curb on a boulevard along the Seine and announced, "Here we are, folks, at the museum of the history of the sewers of Paris. Although our city is compact—only a few miles across—there are today more than 2,100 kilometers of sewer tunnels running under it. That's more than 1,300 miles. Stretched end-to-end, these tunnels would reach from Paris to Istanbul.

"I see it's raining harder now. So please take an umbrella as you leave the van. The entrance is up the blue-railed ramp just to your right as you get off. Take another 45 minutes and see a real section of working sewer and exhibits that will tell you more than you ever wanted to know about waste disposal, yesterday, today and tomorrow. I'll meet you right here at 4:30 to return you to your hotels."

---

1. Counts, Cats, Pigs and Rats
2. The Sewers of Paris

As he passed by the driver, Luigi asked quietly so that nobody else could hear, "Are there really rats down there?"

"Yes, indeed, there are. I promise you'll see at least three or four."

Luigi, last in line leaving the van, asked again, "How big are they? I mean, are they a whole lot bigger than me?"

Philip laughed. "No, they're not even half your size."

Luigi stood as tall as he could. "*Merci,*"[3] he said, heaving a sigh and jumping down to the curb where Luisa was waiting for him.

Luisa was curious, "What were you talking to Philip about, Luigi?"

"Oh, we were talking about rats. He says there are some as big as hippopotamuses. Even bigger. Let's go see them."

✳ ✳ ✳

Carlos' Suite. Paris Ritz Hotel

Refreshed and mostly awake, Carlos reached for the ringing phone.

"*Oui,*"[4] he said simply.

"Carlos, this is the Count Freidrich von Stuffel. You remember me, I trust?"

"Of course, Count. How can I help you today?"

"How's the plan going, Carlos?" the count asked. "Are you going to be ready in time?"

"Everything's right on schedule, Sir," Carlos reassured his latest employer.

---

3. "Thank you."
4. "Yes."

"You know how important this is to me. Personally, I mean. We simply cannot fail," the count said with urgency.

Carlos felt insulted. But he remembered the 5,000,000 Euros in time to check his anger.

"Carlos does not fail, Count," he said tersely. "You checked my references. Don't worry. Carlos' plan will work. Just as it's supposed to."

"It must, Carlos. But what was that business earlier this morning in Casablanca? I know it was your doing even though the authorities claim to be clueless so far. Why did you blow up the Foreign Legion barracks? Not that I mind seeing the French suffer a bit," the count added.

Irritated, Carlos said, "That was step one, Count. I told you there would be a first step offshore, didn't I? Casablanca was a diversion. Simple as that."

"Fine, Carlos, but for the money I'm paying you, I need more information. A few details. Is that asking too much? I mean, 5,000,000 Euros is not a small amount. Am I right?"

"You are right that the amount is not small," Carlos said. "For a small amount, you hire a small-time operator. To employ Carlos, the best of the best, you must pay a higher price. And Carlos doesn't share details of his work with anybody. For any amount of money. Are we clear on that, Count?"

"I understand I've hired the best, Carlos," the count replied. "But surely you'd be willing to give me some idea of how you're planning to proceed. Would you do that for an extra million Euros?"

"Count, Carlos' price is Carlos' price. I have said no amount of money will cause me to go into great detail. You offend me with a mere million Euros more. I will tell you what I'm willing to tell you if that will make you feel better. But not on the telephone. Meet me at the Hemingway Bar in the Ritz Hotel at 4:30 this afternoon. I'll reserve a corner table. The bar will be very busy with self-important souls who will be so wrapped up in talking with one another about their own splendor that no one will be listening.

"But do keep in mind, Count, that once you have any information, you've become a liability for Carlos. You will not be allowed to leak even a hint. Is that understood?"

"Are you threatening me?" the count asked.

"Carlos does not threaten. You've been informed of the cost of the information you seem to need. And you've been told frankly of the consequences of even a whisper of betrayal. It's no more complicated or sinister than that. Just business. I want to be sure we understand each other."

"I believe we have an understanding," the count replied. "I'll see you at 4:30 in the Hemingway Bar. How will I recognize you?"

Carlos smiled to himself. "Most likely I'll be the only puma in the bar. That's a very large and powerful cat, in case you're wondering. If you have problems, just ask the maitre'd for the diamond salesman from South Africa. Do not utter the name 'Carlos.'"

The count interrupted. "You're a cat?" He truly sounded surprised.

"A very big cat," Carlos responded. "Does that trouble you?"

"No. It doesn't trouble me. I just never thought you'd be a . . . puma. That's all."

"Would you feel better," Carlos asked, "if I were to 'meow' for you? Or roar?"

"Cats are fine," the count answered, sounding embarrassed. "I have many friends who are cats, as a matter of fact."

Carlos took charge of the conversation once again, thinking, *The count is too weak and inexperienced to do what he wants to pay someone else to do, but somewhat picky when it comes to trusting a big-time job to a mere cat. And he has no friends who aren't rich and powerful—certainly not cats. How ridiculous.*

"Then one more thing, Count," Carlos said. "At our meeting today, you'll provide proof to me that you've wired half the agreed-upon amount to my accounts in Switzerland and the Caymans. That was our agreement: half upfront, and the other half on completion. I'll expect proof of that, and appreciate it. See you in a few hours."

With that, Carlos put down the phone. He called downstairs for a wake-up call at 3:30 and a reservation for two in the Hemingway Bar at 4:15.

* * *

Le Musée des egouts[5]

"They aren't real, Luigi. They're fakes," Luisa said, irritated with her twin brother.

"Fakes don't blink, Luisa," Luigi insisted. "Or move

---

5. The Sewers Museum

their tails. I saw the one on the left blink and the one in the middle twitched his tail."

"Nonsense!" Luisa insisted. "They're stuffed toys. That's all they are."

Les petits orange tabby gemeaux[6] were standing in the museum of the Paris Sewer System about fifteen meters below the street above. They were looking at a window display containing four rats, each about half the size of the little kittens.

"Anyway," Luigi said, "Philip said we'll probably see rats as big as baby elephants. Those four are just pipsqueaks. Let's keep looking."

Cincinnati wandered up to where the twins were scanning the underground tunnel for bigger rats. He began to tell them about what they were seeing.

"Listen up, you two. You're in a very famous place here. The first sewers in Paris, more than 800 years ago, ran down the middle of the streets that had just been paved with bricks. Some of those bricks are still right in the same place today, but the sewers then were just open ditches in the middle of the streets.

"It wasn't until 600 years later, 200 years ago, when an emperor named Napoleon was in charge, and the construction on these underground tunnels began. More and more of them have been built every year. No other city has a sewer system like the one you're in right now."

Luigi paid rapt attention, but Luisa was bored and looked for a chance to escape from Cincinnati's mini-lecture.

---

6. The tiny orange tabby twins

"What's that big thing over there?" Luigi pointed as Luisa slipped away to join Dusty and Buzzer a little farther down the tunnel they were in.

"That, my little friend," Cincinnati went on, enjoying his temporary role as teacher, "is a 'flushing boat.' There are lots of them. They travel through the sewer tunnels to keep the silt and sediment from building up and slowing the flow of the wastewater. See how fast it's running?" Cincinnati pointed to a metal grate under which a swift stream was moving. And that giant wood and metal ball over there does a similar job."

Luigi turned to look at the giant ball in an alcove ahead of him and Cincinnati.

"So they drag that ball along through the tunnels to keep them cleared out?" Luigi asked. He seemed fascinated by sewer tunnel engineering.

"Right you are, Luigi." Cincinnati grinned.

"What about all those pipes hanging up there off the ceiling?" Luigi continued.

"Some of them carry drinking water to the homes and businesses of Paris," Cincinnati said, "and some hold electrical cables and natural gas lines to send energy to those same homes and businesses," Cincinnati answered.

"I bet they don't have to dig up the streets very often to fix things that are broken," Luigi observed. "They can just come down into one of these sewer tunnels and work right here. Underground. Almost anywhere in the city.

"*Sacre bleu,*"[7] Luigi observed.

"A clever plan for sure, Luigi," Cincinnati agreed. 'And over there . . ." he began to explain something else, but the little kitten had vanished almost instantly.

Cincinnati saw that Luigi had wandered off down the tunnel, peering at the running water below. The dancing pig thought, *I guess he must have learned what he wanted to know. And now he's off scouting for some of those rats he thinks are down here.*

✻   ✻   ✻

Back at the Georges Cinq Hotel

Their afternoon tour complete, the four Texas cats and the dancing pig from Ohio came back to their suite in the famous Georges Cinq Hotel and resumed their disguises as British royalty.

Luigi and Luisa, aka Nick and Nikki, talked among themselves, trying to devise a way to get another order of chocolate cake and vanilla ice cream from room service without Dusty's finding out about it, of course.

Luisa gave their hastily-concocted plan a shot. Turning to Dusty she said in her most tired voice,

---

7. A French exclamation of surprise or amazement. Literally, "Blue blood."

"Dusty Louise, why don't you and Buzzer and Cincinnati go out to dinner at a nice restaurant—and just stop by McDonald's and bring Luigi and me a Big Mac and some fries. We're too tired to do another thing. But we are a little hungry."

She smiled weakly at Dusty and dropped her eyelids to half-mast, as if she were sleepy.

Dusty, used to the twins' occasional scams, wasn't fooled for a minute. "Nice try, you two, but our cousin *René Fopaux* and his assistant *Guy Gondeaux* will be coming by in about half an hour to begin getting ready for Carlos' arrival. We have a plan to develop. You know that very well. *Guy* and *René* are bringing pizzas so we can have our dinner while we work."

Dusty smiled a "gotcha" smile and added with a wink, "Besides, you don't really think the wicked queen is dumb enough to leave the two of you with a phone to call room service for chocolate cake and ice cream, do you?"

Luigi and Luisa shrugged, blinked innocently, and pretended to try to stay awake.

Luisa, ever in character, turned to Luigi. "*Petit frère*,"[8] she said, stifling a pretend yawn, "I guess we better take a quick nap so we'll be ready to work, don't you?"

"Absolutely, *petite soeur*,"[9] Luigi answered. I'm really sleepy."

---

8. "Little brother"
9. "little sister"

The two of them fell into their little bed, put their heads down on *oreillers*,[10] pulled a *drap*[11] up to their chins and pretended to go instantly to sleep.

Luisa whispered to Luigi, "You know there are rats in this hotel, don't you? And some of them are bigger than the customs agent's nose." They both buried their faces in their *oreiller*, laughing hysterically, and hoping Dusty wouldn't notice.

What kind of pizzas do you think René and Guy will bring? Will the little group in the suite be able to devise a plan to capture Carlos once and for all before he can do some terrible thing in Paris? What do you think the count wants him to do, and why? Do you think the count might not trust Carlos now that he knows the puma's a big cat?

---

10. pillows
11. sheet

Parlez Vous Francais?
by Cincinnati

Now that you have a good idea of what to wear, and what to call what you wear, *Apprenona les noms en français de plusieurs members de votre famille.*[12]

English	French	Say It Like This
mother	*mère*	MAIR
father	*père*	PAIR
grandmother	*grandmère*	GRAH(n) mair
grandfather	*grandpère*	GRAH(n) pair
brother	*frère*	FRAIR
sister	*soeur*	SEUHR
aunt	*tante*	TAH(n) teh
uncle	*oncle*	OHN-cleh
male cousin	*cousin*	coo-SZAH(n)
female cousin	*cousine*	coo-SZEE(n)

12. Let's learn the French names for members of your family.

* Chapter 10 *
Pizza, Projets ... et ... Gitans, Gitans, Gitans[1]

In the Suite at the Georges Cinq Hotel

Luigi and Luisa both woke from a short nap to the sound of a sharp rapping on the door of their suite and the smell of melted cheese and Italian herbs.

"Pizza time!" Luigi announced loudly enough for everyone in the room to hear.

"No. Planning time with pizza," Dusty Louise corrected him, equally loud.

Buzzer's cousin *René Fopaux*, complete with his ever-present red beret and his ever-loyal assistant *Guy Gondeaux*, popped into the room with a stack of four pizza boxes.

"Didn't know for sure what you preferred, so we got one all-cheese, one with pineapple and green peppers, one with mushrooms and onions, and one with sardines. Surely that will please everyone's palate," *Guy* announced.

---

1. Pizza, Planning . . . and . . . Gypsies, Gypsies, Gypsies

"Let's eat first while the pizza's hot," *René* suggested to the delight of the twins, whose sugar-high from *un déjeuner de gâteau au chocolat et glace à la vanille*[2] had worn off by now. They were hungry. "Then we can try to figure out what to do with Carlos when he gets to Paris tomorrow morning."

Buzzer added, "While we're eating our pizzas, *René*, why don't Cincinnati and I tell you about Carlos the puma? Just so you and your associates can understand better what we're up against?"

"Good, cousin," *René* answered, "Although we are surely accustomed to dealing with criminals, from petty pickpockets to foreign spies."

Cincinnati stifled a laugh and said, "We certainly don't doubt the abilities of *Brigade Criminelle, René*. But Carlos fits into no category of criminal you've ever come up against. As you probably know, most criminals are clever, but not so smart. And they have few resources to help them plan their activities.

"Carlos, however," Cincinnati continued, "is both smart and clever. And he has resources many governments would be jealous of. Manpower through a worldwide network of freelance confederates and paid full-time assistants. Carlos is rich beyond the wildest dreams of anyone in this room, for sure. He

---

2. a lunch of chocolate cake and vanilla ice cream

uses only the best equipment his money can buy on the black market and the open market. He was trained by the best—the KGB, the Taliban, even Al Qaeda, itself. In short, *il est un mesquin scooter.*"[3]

Guy Gondeaux looked even more perplexed than usual.

"*Que veus-tu dire, Cincinnati?*[4] What is a 'mean motor scooter?'" *Guy* just had to ask.

And Luigi had to answer first, before Cincinnati or anyone else could. "He means Carlos is fast, powerful and up to no good," Luigi said, looking to Buzzer and the dancing pig to see if he got the answer right.

"That's pretty good, Luigi," Buzzer said to the little kitten's everlasting delight. Turning to *Guy* and *René*, he added, "Carlos is a prototype gold-plated sociopath. He has never stolen a penny from anybody. He doesn't carry a gun or a knife and would never get into a fight with another creature. Those things he considers bad—even criminal."

He went on, "But when it comes to his work, he thinks nothing of blowing an airliner out of the skies or bombing a building or poisoning a city's water supply. To him, as long as he's being paid to do these things, those responsible are the ones paying him. He thinks he's only doing his job."

"Not much conscience, huh?" *René* asked.

"No conscience at all when he's being paid to do a job," Cincinnati answered, adding, "but if he's not being paid, he wouldn't harm a housefly."

"This is a very strange character, *René* commented. "Strange, indeed. What more can you tell us, Buzzer?"

---

3. "He's a mean motor scooter."
4. "What do you mean, Cincinnati?"

"Only two things: first, Carlos is a master of disguise. He may appear as a Chinese shoe salesman, a Swiss watch salesman, a Russian caviar salesman, even. Last week in Buenos Aires, he was a children's rocking horse salesman. So he's always *a marchand,*[5] but from where and selling what—who knows?"

At the word "knows," Luigi and Luisa burst into gales of laughter, spraying bits of cheese and sardines across the room.

Remembering the now-jailed customs agent, *René* joined in their laughter. *Guy* simply looked confused. As usual.

René turned to Buzzer. "You said there were two more things to know about this Carlos the puma. The first was his many disguises. What is the second?"

Buzzer leaned forward. "Here is what makes him so hard to catch, *René.* He is a master of misdirection. Every time you think you've figured out his next move, suddenly you find you're not only on the wrong track, but you're *really* wrong. And he does strange little things to divert your attention from what he's really up to."

"I think I understand, Buzz, but could you give me an example or two? Just to be sure I've got the right idea," *René* asked.

Buzzer turned to the dancing pig. "Cincinnati, you want to take a shot at this one?"

Cincinnati nodded, but before he could answer, Luisa piped up, "Like last week, cousin *René,* on his way from the prison he'd just escaped from in Brazil, he blew up a ciga-

---

5. salesman

rette boat on the Amazon River and, an hour later, blew up the docks at a town called Marañon a little farther down the river."

"Both for no good reason," Luigi added. "And I'll bet you a piece of chocolate cake and two scoops of vanilla ice cream that he'll do something crazy on his way from Brazil to France.

"Just for the halibut," Luigi added, looking at Dusty to see if he was going to get by with that little transgression.

She frowned, but let it pass.

Guy, however, burst into raucous laughter.

Luisa and Luigi looked at him, each wondering if he really got the pun, or just found something funny that nobody else noticed.

René began to sum up. "So we have a smart and clever criminal who will likely disguise himself as a salesman, but we don't know a salesman of what? Or where he will claim to be coming from. He'll try to lead us astray with meaningless diversions, while planning to do whatever it is he is coming to Paris to do. He has limitless resources and lots of assistants."

"Hmmm. Do we know enough about anything to create a plan to stop him?" Buzzer wondered.

"Luigi, do you and Luisa want to give *René* and *Guy* your little speech about how to plan for Carlos?"

Luigi nodded to Luisa as if to say, "Your turn."

"We have to think like a criminal," she said. "A terrorist. An assassin. We have to get our heads into being Carlos the puma and imagine what he's likely to be coming here to do. And then we have to come up with a spectacularly clever plan that's sure to stop him. It won't be easy, but we have some experience. Right, Luigi?" She turned to her twin brother.

"*Tu a reson, Luisa,*"[6] he answered. "We simply have to become Carlos the puma."

"Let's get to work, then," Dusty said as she cleared away mostly empty pizza boxes while Cincinnati and Buzzer arranged chairs around a round table in the parlor of their suite.

* * *

The Next Afternoon—In the Paris Ritz's Hemingway Bar

The room was semi-dark as Count Freidrich von Stuffel approached the maitre'd. "*Bon aprés-midi, Monsieur,*"[7] the count said. "I'm to meet the diamond salesman from South Africa here right about now. Can you direct me to him, please?"

"But of course, sir," the maitre'd answered. "He's waiting for you at the table in the back corner—away from all the hubbub. Follow me, please."

The maitre'd led the count through small tables past the bar and into a cramped alcove in a corner near the back of the room.

Seeing Carlos sitting alone, his back to an outside wall, the maitre'd said, "Your guest has arrived *Monsieur Vendeur de Diamants.*"[8] He pulled out and offered the count a chair across the little table from Carlos, then turned and left.

---

6. "You're right, Luisa."
7. "Good afternoon, Sir."
8. "Mister Diamond Salesman."

"You really are a cat!" the count said, looking across the table at Carlos.

"Carlos does not lie to his clients, Count. I told you I am a puma. And now you see for yourself that I am, in fact, a large and powerful cat. I ask you once again, 'Does that trouble you?'"

The count locked eyes with Carlos. Seeing the steely and steady bead of the puma's eyes, he blinked, "I told you not two hours ago it is of no concern to me whether you are a cat or a green-striped gorilla, Carlos. Just as long as you get the job done for me. That's all that I'm concerned about. "Now, what about your plan? How will you proceed?"

Carlos leaned back in his chair as if to put the count on notice that he would not be questioned or intimidated. "First things first, Count. Would you like a drink? Or a snack, perhaps? I've ordered two Coca-Cola® Zeros and a bottle of Evian® water. If that's not to your liking, we can get whatever you'd prefer."

"That will be fine, I'm sure, Carlos. Now about your plan. When will you get started?" The count seemed to be in a hurry.

But Carlos would not be hurried. Not by the likes of this "count," anyway.

The big cat once again smiled. "Please do not question me, Count. I've told you I'll tell you what I intend to tell you, and nothing more. But our discussion cannot begin until you've shown me proof that half the agreed-upon price has already been forwarded to my accounts in Zurich and the Caymans. I trust you're prepared to do that?"

The count reached into his pocket, but pulled his hand back to the table quickly as a waiter walked up with four glasses of ice, two bottles of Coca-Cola Zero, a bottle of Evian and a small dish each of assorted nuts and various kinds of olives. He set them down in front of Carlos and the count, then turned and left without speaking.

Count von Stuffel again reached into his coat and pulled out two flimsies, each a telegraphed receipt. One was for 1,000,000 Euros, and the other 1,500,000 Euros, the first to Carlos' account in Switzerland and the other to another of his accounts in the Caymans.

Handing them across the table to Carlos, he asked, "What if you fail, Carlos? Do I get this money back?"

The big puma bristled. "First, I will not fail. Carlos has never failed, and he will never fail. Second, just to be sure we understand one another, the answer would be 'absolutely not.' This money is gone forever, as far as you're concerned. And now, I have a question for you since you seem to lack some trust in the reputation of Carlos, the best of the best."

Staring menacingly, Carlos asked, "Besides, when I succeed, as I always do, how do I know you will honor your agreement and pay me the second half?"

This time the count bristled. "The Count von Stuffel pays those who work for him according to their agreements. You finish the job, you will get the money. Have no concern, Carlos."

"Oh, I'm not particularly concerned, Count. I'm sure while you were checking me out you also learned it does not pay to cross Carlos. The few who have tried are, shall we say, permanently regretful. As a matter of fact, as soon as I'm finished with this little job for you, I have a score to settle with the only ones who have ever crossed Carlos. Not once, but twice now. A certain undercover cat and pig will be hearing from me shortly. The day after *Le jour de la Bastille*."[9]

Pouring himself some of both the Evian and the Coca-Cola Zero and putting a few of the olives and cashews on his small plate, the count again asked, "Now will you tell me whatever it is you're willing to say, Carlos?"

"First," Carlos answered, "I must know from you why this job is so important to you. Personally, that is. Then I'll decide how much of my plan I can trust you with."

"All right, here it is. Plain and simple. About one hun-

---

9. *Bastille* Day. July 14th in France. Equivalent to July 4 Independence Day in the U.S.

dred forty years ago, in the 1870s, my grandfather's grandfather was Franz Joseph, leader of the Austro-Hungarian
Empire. Like most of us in what is now Europe, at the time
he was, shall we say, less than enchanted with the French.
In return for an unprovoked and odious attack launched
by the French, Franz Joseph laid siege to Paris. Within
weeks, he had strangled the city, bringing it to its knees.
The people of Paris were reduced to eating rats. There was
no other food allowed to be brought into the city.

"Believing he had made his point and not wishing to
create a famine, my ancestor simply withdrew his troops
and went home. But true to form, the French, though
soundly beaten, simply declared victory. And in thanks-
giving for this *fausse victoire*,[10] raised millions of Francs and
built the target—your job. In celebration, Carlos, for a victory that was not a victory at all. The whole thing was most
shameful to the benevolent real victors, the empire of my
ancestors. It shames me to this day, I tell you."

The count concluded, "When I first heard the story
from my grandfather, I was a small child in Prussia. My
ancestor could have brought Paris to its knees, but he chose
instead to show them mercy, I vowed to avenge the insult."

He paused, his face serious. "And that's what I'm paying
you to help me do today."

The count tossed two olives and three cashews into his
mouth, took a long pull on his drink, sat back and sighed as
if he'd just run a 100-meter dash.

Carlos had been listening patiently. He thought the

---

10. fake, or phony victory

count was perhaps a bit off his rocker, harboring a grudge for five or six generations. But, for Carlos, business is business.

"Very well, Count. I understand your reasons. Now I know the target and why it is the target. In return, here's what I'll tell you. And this is all I'll tell you about my plan.

"It will all take place on *Bastille* Day, July 14th. That's just a few days from now, no? And there will be distractions. Diversions all over the city. But only one will be the real target. And only one will be hit by real explosives. You know which one." Carlos had said all he wanted to say.

But the count had not heard nearly enough. Not yet.

"How can you do that, Carlos?"

"Do what, Count?"

"Create so many diversions and still destroy the real target . . . all in one day?"

"Oh, it will take only hours. Perhaps as few as three or four," Carlos answered, ready to end this conversation.

"I don't understand, Carlos," the count insisted. "You can't be in so many places at once, can you?"

"Of course not. Don't be ridiculous. Carlos has help. Lots of help."

"Before we take another step, I must know the nature of this help. Who will be working with you?"

"Count von Stuffel, you are making your liability bigger with each question. I'll answer this question, and then I am through talking to you. Only contact me if you wish to call off the job and pay me the other half of my fee as well," Carlos said firmly.

"Agreed," the count quickly responded. "Now tell me. Who will help you?'

Carlos leaned halfway across the table and almost whispered, "Gypsies. A team of a dozen Gypsies."

The Hungarian Count almost came out of his chair. He said only one word. "Perfect," he said.

Then he stood and quietly left the Hemingway Bar. Carlos watched him walk the long, blue-carpeted corridor to the front door and disappear onto the *place énorme*[11] in front to the Paris Ritz.

Do you think the four Texas cats and the dancing pig have convinced René *that Carlos is not just your average criminal? Will the* Brigade Criminelle *be able to help capture Carlos before he can strike the target for the count? What do you think that target might be? And what will a dozen Gypsies be doing to help Carlos? Does Count Freidrich von Stuffel already know too much? Will he leak some of what he knows?*

---

11. enormous plaza

Parlez Vous Francais?
by Cincinnati

Now that you know the words for the members of your family, nous allons apprendre plus de mots, cette fois—ci a propos " être dans un hôtel."[12]

English	French	Say It Like This
hotel	hotel	OH-tel
lobby	vestibule	vehs-teh-BUEHL
clerk	concierge	con-see-AIRZH
bellman	groom d'hotel	gruhm deh OH-tel
elevator	ascenseur	ah-sah(n)-SEUHR
single room	chambre simple	SHAHM-breh SAHM-pleh
double room	chambre double	SHAHM-breh DOO-bleh
suite	suite	suite
room service	service de chambre	sahr-VEESZ deh SHAHM-breh
bathroom	salle de bain	sahl-deh BAH(n)
towels	serviettes	sahr-vee-EHT
sheets	draps	DRAH
pillows	oreillers	ohr-vee-YEA
wakeup call	reveil	reh-VEAH
restaurant	restaurant	rehs-tah-RAH(n)
coffee shop	café	cah-FAY
gift shop	boutique de cadeaux	boo-TEEK deh cah-DOH

---

12. We are going to learn some more words—this time about staying in a hotel.

Part Three

The Monuments of Paris

"Carlos may very well be smart and clever, have a lot of resources and helpers all over the place, but the four Texas cats and the dancing pig will take him down. We're smart and clever, too. And we have the resources of Cats In Action behind us and the help of the whole *Brigade Criminelle*. Carlos is toast."

—Dusty Louise
Big Sister, Detective and
Pilot-in-Training

* Chapter 11 *
Lumiéres brillantes de la tour *Eiffel* et les plans secrets dans la nuit[1]

Back in the Suite at the Georges Cinq Hotel

As *René* and *Guy* were leaving the room to contact French Intelligence, the former *Deuxiéme*, Luigi and Luisa pulled their cousin wearing the red beret aside in the hallway.

"We're working on a plan of our own" Luigi said, "to start up once we think we know who may have hired Carlos. We'll tell you all about it in the morning if you can come a half-hour early for breakfast. Can you do that? Without bringing *Guy* or telling Buzzer?"

"*Oui, je peus fair cela,*"[2] *René* answered. "But why don't you want Buzzer or Cincinnati or Dusty to know?"

---

1. Bright Eiffel Lights and Secret Plans in the Night
2. "Yes, I can do that."

"Because we don't want them getting into it until we're ready to talk about it," Luisa answered. "If we don't come up with a great idea tonight after they go to sleep, it wouldn't be good for Dusty, especially, to know anything about what we're up to. She'd just claim we're wasting time, or being silly, or not sleeping when we're supposed to."

Luigi jumped in. "And if we think we have a great idea, we want to run it by you first. So you can say you like it in front of everybody else. Kind of support us, if you know what I mean."

René said, "*Je comprens ce que tu es en train de dire,*[3] but why not include Buzzer, too? Early in the morning, I mean?"

Luisa answered, "Our brother is our hero. He's a legend on six continents. One of the reasons he's so famous is that he always tells the truth. We can't—no, won't—ever ask him to ever fib to Dusty. That would be wrong." She smiled at *René.*

"We don't mind fibbing a bit ourselves, though," Luigi added. "If a little white lie will help us catch Carlos faster, we're up for it. Or even a whopper monster of a lie. Any time."

"We prefer to call it simple misdirection—the same thing that's made Carlos famous and kept him out of jail," Luisa explained. "We just want to stay out of trouble. That's all. Or at least we want to stay out of Dusty Louise's sights."

René chuckled. "So you don't mind if I have to compromise the truth a bit, eh?"

---

3. "I understand what you're saying."

"Well, I guess we never looked at it that way. But, c'mon Cousin *René*, you're French, after all. What does it matter to you?" Luigi responded.

René Francois Fopaux, head of the world-famous *Brigade Criminelle*, roared with laughter so loud, in fact, that Dusty hurried over to see what was going on.

"What's so funny, *René*?" she asked, impatient as usual.

René answered, "These two were just telling me about some American hillbillies. I think you call them Ma and Pa Kettle."

Luigi smiled at Luisa and gave her a high-four.

René returned the salute with two dewclaws up. Then he turned and walked quickly to the elevator, where *Guy Gondeaux* was holding the door open for him.

Back in the suite, the yellow tabby twins were pumped.

"Can we go see the *Eiffel Tower* light up?" Luisa asked Buzzer. "Please."

Luigi added, "Tonight may be our last chance. Once Carlos gets here tomorrow morning, we won't have a minute to spare."

Buzzer looked at a big grandfather clock in the corner just as it started to chime 9;00. "I suppose we have time to go see it. Doesn't it light up until eleven, Cincinnati?"

"Right-o," Cincinnati said, adding, "Since we have plenty of time, why don't we show Dusty and the twins how most of the people of Paris get from one place to another?"

"The Metro?" Buzzer asked, smiling at his pig friend.

"The Metro," Cincinnati answered.

"What's that?" Dusty wanted to know.

Luisa couldn't resist. "*C'est dans le metro.*"[4] Immediately, she knew she shouldn't have answered Dusty's question in French. Dusty just couldn't stand for the twins to know something she didn't.

Dusty turned to Buzzer and Cincinnati with a haughty expression, "Does Luisa have any idea what she's talking about?" she asked "Is this Metro really a subway?"

Luisa kept quiet, pretending to ignore the insult Dusty had flung at her. Luigi shot a quick glance and drew a front paw across his mouth from left to right.

Cincinnati stepped in before a family feud could break out. "The Metro is the subway system in Paris. You can get on at any one of dozens of stations, and you can go almost anywhere in Paris in a matter of minutes. The subway is very fast."

Forgetting her snit at not knowing something Luisa knew, Dusty's curiosity came roaring to the surface. "Where do you get on? Is it safe, even at night? Can we get to the *Eiffel Tower* from here?"

Buzzer knew it was time to slow her down, so he answered slowly, "Just down the block here on *Georges Cinq Boulevard.*[5] *Oui, oui,* even at night. *Et, oui,*[6] we can get to the *Eiffel Tower* easily from here."

Cincinnati added, "But there's a better place to see the lights than right at the tower, itself."

Buzzer nodded, knowing what Cincinnati was about to suggest.

---

4. "It's a subway."
5. George V Boulevard
6. "Yes, yes . . . And, yes,"

"Where?" Dusty was still revved up.

"From the top of the highest point in Paris," the dancing pig answered. "On the steps of *la basilica du Sacre Coeur*[7] in the *Montmartre* district. We'll have to change subway trains a couple of times, but the trains run every few minutes, so it won't take long."

Buzzer looked at Luigi and Luisa. "Are you guys ready for a subway ride and a climb up some steep stairs?"

In unison, they shouted, "*Ouí*!"

★ ★ ★

René and Guy at French Intelligence Bureau

Inspector *Remy Dewclaux*, head of the French Intelligence Service, sank deeply into his big leather chair and sighed, placing his right front paw in front of his lips as if in thought. The inspector, a German shorthaired pointer, was famous for fidgeting. Seems he just couldn't sit still for a minute.

After *René* had told him what he needed from Intelligence, however, *Remy* slipped into a pensive mood, removing his monocle and re-packing his curved briar pipe.

7. Sacred Heart Basilica

"So you are interested in identifying any foreigners who might have come into France in the last few days?" he asked? "There will be thousands, you know."

"Oui, mais c'est même mieux s'ils sont très riches[8] *René* answered. "That will bring the number down to a mere handful. This Carlos the puma doesn't do his work unless somebody, or some organization, is paying him money, and I mean millions of Euros. So if we can discover who his employer is, we'll have a pretty good idea of what his mission might be, *non?*"[9]

"Mais bien sûr"[10] Remy agreed. "Very well, *René*, we'll look for wealthy travelers entering France in the past few days. And we'll put a watch on airport arrivals, train stations and border crossings for the next week—until you tell us to stop. I suppose your group is handling hotels?"

"Oh, yes, *Remy, tous les hotels*[11] are being contacted by a group of agents under the command of my assistant here, *Guy Gondeaux. Guy* and his team will be sure to alert each of the luxury hotels in the city and suburbs to be watching for Carlos. We'll have them call at once if the big puma should register. He turned to his hapless assistant.

"C'est pas vrais, Guy?"[12] *René* asked.

"Certainement, Monsieur,"[13] *Guy* answered, snickering slightly to himself as if something funny had crossed his mind just as he spoke.

---

8. "Yes, but even better if they're very rich"
9. no?
10. "But of course"
11. all the hotels
12. "Right, Guy?"
13. "Certainly, Sir"

"Very well, then," the head of the French Intelligence Service said in a first step toward ending the late-night meeting. Then he added, "Should I contact my counterparts at the C.I.A. in *les Etats Unis*, MI6 *en Angleterre*, or the KGB in *Russie*,[14] do you think, *René*?"

Guy Gondeaux looked up. "That will not be necessary, Sir."

René was surprised to see his assistant offer any opinion about anything at all. *Guy* had never shown any initiative of any kind, on any subject, before. He added quickly, "My cousins and their associate the dancing pig will have informed the secret Central Intelligence Agency at Langley in Virginia, and the even more secret Cats In Action in the White House basement of their actions. If you can reach Boris in Moscow and Sir Clive in London on a secure phone, I think a word to them would probably be wise, *Remy*, but be sure the international press doesn't get onto the story. We don't need that kind of help right now."

"We'll stay in touch, then, *René*," *Remy* promised, removing his monocle and laying it on his desk as he stood to see his visitors to the door.

"*Merci, Remy. Et bonne nuit a toi*,"[15] *René* said as he and *Guy* left the offices of French Intelligence.

✳ ✳ ✳

The Metro on the Way to Sacre Coeur
Cincinnati was telling Dusty and the twins some of the

---

14. United States, England, Russia
15. "Thank you, Remy, and goodnight to you."

ways to avoid problems on the Metro. "First," he said, "never stand close to the door. Standing there will allow thieves to grab something from you just as the train stops and then run out the door and up the stairs to the street."

Luisa looked puzzled. "But we're all sitting down, Cincinnati. Everybody's sitting down. There's nobody standing up anywhere," she said.

"Ah, yes, Luisa," the dancing pig said. "But it's 9:30 at night and the Metro is not too crowded. During the morning and evening rush hours, more people will be standing than sitting, you see."

"What else, Cincinnati?" Dusty wanted to know, adding, "I thought you said the Metro is safe, even at night."

"It is, Dusty, but you have to be careful of pickpockets just the same," Cincinnati answered.

"Can't get me," Luigi piped up. "I don't even have any pockets and neither does Luisa. And we're sitting down nowhere near the doors. Safe as a rat in the sewer, if you ask me."

Luisa, Buzzer and Cincinnati laughed. Dusty, embarrassed as usual at Luigi's behavior, moved across the aisle to an empty seat.

"We get off at the next stop—in *Montmartre*—a couple of blocks from *Sacre Coeur*," Buzzer announced. "Remember, twins, the doors only stay open a few seconds, so don't dilly-dally."

As the train came to a stop and the doors opened. Luigi and Luisa watched with glee as a small, elderly Gypsy lady used the pointed tip of her folded up umbrella to flip a little hat Dusty had bought that afternoon right off her head and into a shopping bag.

"She just nipped Dusty's new hat," Luisa whispered to Luigi as they hopped from the train onto the station's platform.

"I'm not telling Dusty!" Luigi said.

"Me, neither," Luisa answered. "She's going to go bonkers when she figures it out, though."

Do you think the French Intelligence Service will be able to identify a list of rich foreigners who have entered France recently? If they do, will the count's name be on it? And if it is, will the Brigade Criminelle figure out he's the one who's hired Carlos? What about the lights on the Eiffel Tower? Will the Texas cats and the dancing pig be able to see them from the top of the big hill in front of Sacre Coeur Basilica? Will Dusty figure out her new hat is missing, or will Luigi and Luisa have to tell her?

Parlez Vous Francaise?

by Cincinnati

Now that you will know what to say and how to say it when you stay in a French hotel, *apprennons comme on dit les parts de votre corps* [16] in case you need to talk to a doctor. [16]

English	French	Say It Like This
ankles	chevilles	sheh-vee-EH
arms	bras	BRAH
cheeks	joues	ZHOO
chin	menton	MAHN-toh(n)
ears	oreilles	oh-RAY-yuh
eyes	yeux	YEUH
face	visage	vee-SZAHG
fingers	doits	DWAH
hair	cheveaux	SHEH-veau
hands	mains	MAH(n)
head	tête	TEHT
hips	hanches	ANN-szeh
lips	levres	LAY-vreh
mouth	bouche	BOOSZH
neck	cou	COO
shoulders	èpaules	eh-PAHL
toes	orteils	ohr-TEH(l)
tongue	langue	LAHN-geh
wrists	poignets	PWAHN-yeh
stomach	estomac	es-toh-MAH

---

16. Let's learn how to say the parts of your body.

* Chapter 12 *
Guy est le type.
Où bien il est?[1]

The Steps in Front of Sacre Coeur Basilica—10:00 P.M.

"Wow! Look over there to the south!" Luigi was first to spot the flashing lights at the *Eiffel Tower*.

"Looks like a Christmas tree," Luisa added. "We can climb up the *Eiffel Tower*, but we're not supposed to climb in the Christmas tree, right Dusty?"

"No climbing in the tree. Either of you. But, Luigi, how do you know the *Eiffel Tower* is south of us?"

"Easy, big sister," Luigi said. "Three ways: first, my internal magnetometer said I was looking south; second, if I spin around really fast and then stop, I'm always facing east—it happens every time. I can't tell you why; and third, I looked at a map of the Metro system back at the hotel. The *Eiffel Tower* was toward the bottom, and *Sacre Coeur* was toward the top. *Voilá!*[2] We're looking south."

---

1. Guy's the Guy. Or is He?   2. There it is!

Dusty thought with a sigh, *Luigi's still a wise guy, but at least he had the curiosity to look at a map. I wonder if he'll ever grow up?*

Cincinnati told them there were more than 200,000 lights on the *Eiffel Tower.* The four cats and the dancing pig watched for a few minutes as the lights twinkled up and down. After a short time, Luisa faked a yawn and suggested, "We better get on back to the hotel right away. All of us need to get a good night's sleep so we'll be ready in the morning when Carlos gets here."

Luigi, knowing Luisa wanted everyone to go to sleep so the two of them could get started thinking about a humongous, stupendous plan to capture Carlos, added, "Right you are, Luisa. *"J'ai vraiment sommeil."* [3]

Dusty Louise, suspicious that the two kittens were asking to go to sleep, suddenly missed her new hat. *"Ou est mon chapeau?* [4] Does anybody see it? I just bought it this afternoon."

Luigi whispered to Cincinnati, "Luisa and I saw an old Gypsy lady tip it off Dusty's head with her umbrella as we got off the Metro. We didn't tell her because the old lady took off running like a jackrabbit. We couldn't have caught her. Besides, why tempt Dusty to start screaming in the Metro station?"

Smiling, Cincinnati turned to Dusty. "Maybe you left it at the hotel, Dusty. Or maybe one of those famous pickpockets took it off your head in the Metro."

"Don't be ridiculous, Cincinnati," Dusty said. "Nobody

---

3. "I'm really sleepy."
4. "Where's my hat?"

could take a hat off my head without my knowing it immediately."

Luisa grinned, and she and Luigi started down the long, steep stairway in front of the Church, headed for the Metro and the 20-minute ride back to their hotel.

* * *

Back in the Suite at the Georges Cinq—1:00 A.M.

Everybody but the twins had been asleep for a couple of hours. Holding the cordless phone's receiver, Luisa quietly slipped out the door and into the hallway. She quickly dialed the all-night room service number.

"Ah, yes," she said with a British accent softly into the phone when the *service de chambre*[5] answered. "This is the Duchess Fiona Welch in room 435. We require two servings of chocolate cake and vanilla ice cream, *s'il vous plait,*[6] for Nick and Nikki, the twins from Oxford. They're frightfully hungry all the time, you see, and wide awake right now, demanding a substantial snack. Add five Euros for the bellman, and charge it to Sir Clive's account."

She thought briefly, then added, "Also, room service, please ask the bellman who brings it up to rap once lightly on our door and just leave the tray beside our door. We don't want to wake everyone, now do we? Thank you ever so much."

She smiled as she slipped back into the suite where she and Luigi were putting the finishing touches on their grandiose plan for capturing Carlos.

---

5. room service
6. please (if you please, literally)

"You think we're on the right track?" Luigi asked as Luisa slipped back into her little rollaway bed in the dark parlor.

"Nobody else has a plan, do they?" she answered. "I think this just might work. That *Guy's* not as dumb as everyone seems to think he is. I'm sure of it. And, besides, who would ever suspect him of anything? He'll do exactly as he's told, and he won't think too much for himself—the perfect agent, don't you think?"

Just as she finished her question, the twins heard a single soft rap on the door. Slipping quietly to the hallway, they found their reward—two servings, which they brought back quietly to their beds and began to eat slowly, savoring every mouthful.

✳ ✳ ✳

The Next Afternoon at the Paris Ritz Hotel

Carlos the puma, having dismissed his client, the Count von Stuffel, went back to his suite intent on finishing the nap the count had interrupted a couple of hours earlier. No sooner had he lay down on the king-size bed than the phone rang again.

"*Allò,*"[7] Carlos barked into the receiver.

"Mr. Diamond Salesman, this is the *concierge*[8] desk downstairs, sir. There are three gentlemen here asking for you." He was speaking softly so nobody but Carlos could hear him.

---

7. "Hello"
8. A French word commonly used in English. It means "caretaker" or "head bellman."

Carlos asked, "Are they my pilots and driver?"

The concierge hesitated. "No, Sir, I don't think so. At least I wouldn't personally want to be in any airplane they might be flying."

"Ah, the Gypsies, then," Carlos said.

"Most assuredly," he whispered. "They definitely are Gypsies. Do you wish to see them, Sir? You can turn your television control to channel 14 and you will be able to see me, my desk and those who are asking for you."

Carlos had learned early in his career that it's always good to be cautious. He flipped on the TV and punched up channel 14. Looking at the three scruffy characters waiting with the concierge, he recognized the part-time employees he had worked with several times in the past.

"If you will—please bring them to my suite in the service elevator," he said to the concierge. "Send up some bottled water, a bottle of Bordeaux with glasses and a few snacks—olives, nuts, that kind of thing, please. And when we're finished here, I'll call you to ask for the winner of today's cricket match between Islamabad and Abu Dhabi. That'll be your sign to come back to accompany these guests downstairs and out the back door."

* * *

An Early Breakfast with René at the Georges Cinq Hotel

"So that's our big idea, *René*, Luisa said. "What do you think?"

René, who had come alone and early to meet with Luigi and Luisa as they had asked, sat back in his chair in the elegant coffee shop and stroked his chin with his left front paw. "I have mixed feelings, *petits chats*.[9] "The plan is ingenious, no doubt about that. I congratulate you both on sound thinking and good planning strategy. My only concern is the role you're suggesting for my assistant, *Guy Gondeaux*. *Guy* is a few bricks shy of a load, as you Americans might say. Somewhat stupid, actually."

"That's what makes him almost perfect for the job, *René*," Luigi countered. "Has he ever failed to do exactly what you asked him to do?"

"Never. He always follows directions precisely," *René* answered.

Luisa added, "Does he try to think too much for himself? Act on his own in doing anything?"

René leaned forward and smiled. "No," he said. "I have only seen him speak one time without being asked, or even prompted. That was last night at our meeting with French Intelligence. He seemed not to want your Central Intelligence Agency, Britain's MI6 or the KGB to know about our efforts to track down Carlos the puma. I must admit I found that strange. And out of character for him."

"We don't think *Guy's* as dimwitted as he pretends to be," Luisa said. "That blank look on his face and those odd little laughs he lets out once in awhile—they seem practiced to us. It's as though he wants others to think he's dumb."

"You may both be right. For someone who seems to be— shall we say—a little goofy, *Guy* is quite capable, even precise, about doing exactly what I tell him to do. That makes

---

9. kittens

him valuable to me," *René* said, and added, "So let's try your plan. It might just work."

Just then Buzzer, Cincinnati and Dusty rushed into the coffee shop.

"There you two are," Dusty said with a scowl. "We've been looking all over for you."

"We were here with *René*," Luisa said innocently. "We woke up early, and we were hungry, so we came on to the coffee shop for some milk. Then our cousin came in. So we've been talking about this and that."

"I guess you didn't hear us last night when we told you that if we woke up early, we'd meet you in the coffee shop," Luigi added.

"How could you be hungry?" Dusty wanted to know. "I saw your tray and the empty cake and ice cream dishes in the hallway outside our door."

"We saw those, too," Luisa said.

"And we wished they were still full," Luigi added.

Cincinnati, glancing at a CNN Worldwide news report, interrupted. "Carlos has struck. It's on CNN right now." He pointed to the wall-mounted television. "About a half hour ago, a bomb destroyed the barracks of the French Foreign Legion in Casablanca. It had to be Carlos on his way here."

"That explains the stop in Marrakech," Buzzer said. "Typical Carlos. Stops in Marrakech, drives to Casablanca and back, then gets on his plane headed for Paris so he's in the air when the barracks blow up. Now he can claim he stopped in Marrakech to refuel and take a nap, and that he was nowhere near Casablanca when the bomb went off."

"That means he must be almost here," *René* suggested. "Very clever, indeed."

"You do have agents at the airports, right?" Cincinnati asked *René*.

"Yes, and *Guy* has a team covering each of the luxury hotels. Maybe we can find him before he even gets settled in," *René* said hopefully.

"Don't count on it," Cincinnati shot back. "He's a slippery one, for sure."

✳ ✳ ✳

In Carlos' Suite at the Paris Ritz

Carlos opened his door when the concierge knocked, welcoming three shady-looking characters into his suite, along with a bellman rolling a cart with drinks and snacks on it.

"Put it by the window," Carlos said, handing the bellman five Euros. "I'll roll it into the hallway when our meeting's finished, and you can pick it up later."

Without waiting to be asked, the three Gypsies helped themselves to the contents of the rolling cart. Each grabbed a glass and a plate and filled them with goodies.

"*Servez vous*,"[10] Carlos said belatedly. "Enjoy the refreshments, and then we'll get down to business. We have much to discuss this afternoon."

✳ ✳ ✳

Back in the Coffee Shop at the Georges Cinq Hotel

"So that's our idea. We'll turn *Guy* into a double agent

---

10. "Help yourselves."

and plant him next to Carlos' employer, whoever that turns out to be," Luisa concluded. She had explained the grandiose plan she and Luigi had hatched during the night while everybody else ate their breakfasts.

"*Que penses tu?*"[11] Luigi directed his question to *René*.

"It's an excellent plan. *Je penses que ça va marcher,*"[12] *René* answered, right on cue.

Buzzer spoke up. "It's a sound plan, but I have a question or two." Turning to *René*, he asked, "Do you trust this assistant of yours? And do you think he's the right one for the job? Frankly he seems a little shy of brainpower to me."

"Trust him? I think so, Buzz. He's never given me any reason not to. Is he right for the job? Seems to me he's just about perfect. Luisa and Luigi figured out that he will follow my directions to the letter. And he certainly won't take it upon himself to try to do anything on his own—without asking me first." *René* thought a minute, then he said, "Yes, Buzz, I'd say he's not only the right one for the job, but likely the perfect one. I can control him." *René* winked at the twins as if they had a secret from the others.

And, of course, they did.

Do you think there's a tiny chance that Luigi and Luisa fooled Dusty with their middle-of-the-night cake and ice cream? Will Guy be able to do the job Luigi and Luisa have planned for him? Do you think he can be trusted? And who are the three scruffy-looking Gypsies who are about to meet with Carlos? What part do you think they'll play in his plan? And just what is his plan, anyway?

---

11. "What do you think?"
12. I think it will work.

Parlez Vous Francais?
by Cincinnati

Now you can speak a little French. Let's learn some more – *Cette fois-ci les mots journaliers qui vous avait besoin de connaître concernant la nourriture.*[13]

English	French	Say It Like This
breakfast	*petit–déjeuner*	peh-TEE-deh-ZHE-NAY
lunch	*déjeuner*	deh-zhe-NAY
dinner	*dîners*	dee-NAY
snack	*casse-croûte*	cahs-CROOT
table	*table*	TAH-bleh
chair	*siège*	see-EHGZ
dining room	*salle a manger*	sahl ah mahn-ZHAY
kitchen	*cusine*	cue-SZEE(n)
plate	*plat*	PLAH
cup	*tasse*	TAHS
glass	*verre*	VEHR
knife	*couteau*	COO-toh
fork	*fourchette*	fohr-SZEHT
spoon	*cuillère*	CUE-yair
napkin	*serviette*	SAIR-vyet
bowl	*bol*	BOHL
tablecloth	*nappe*	NAHP

---

13. This time about everyday words you'll need to know concerning eating.

* Chapter 13 *

Une douzaine de gitans et une bref liste des Visiteurs riches[1]

In Carlos' Suite Again at the Paris Ritz Hotel

"Have each of you recruited three trustworthy assistants?" Carlos asked the trio of Gypsies who were busily eating snacks and drinking wine in his suite. He looked at each of them. "Emile, how about you?"

"*Oui, trois homes valides,*"[2] Emile answered between bites of olives.

"Francois?" Carlos asked.

"*Monsieur, toutes les trois sont des femmes,*"[3] Francois replied.

"Franz?" Carlos asked the third Gypsy.

"*Deux de mes frères et ma soeur,*"[4] Franz answered.

"You must be sure each of them is completely depend-

---

1. A Dozen Gypsies and a Short List of Rich Visitors
2. "Yes, three good men."
3. "Yes, Sir. All three are women."
4. "Two of my brothers and my sister."

able. Our timetable will be precise, and I can tolerate no mistakes. Do you understand that?" Carlos narrowed his eyes at them to be sure his point was made.

"*Bien, alors.*[5] You may tell each of them their future depends on following directions precisely. If someone makes a mistake, I'll be able to tell immediately. If it is one of your assistants, both of you will not be paid the second two-thirds of your fees. Everybody understand this?"

"Now, are there any questions?" Carlos asked, testing to see if these three "supervisors" were clever enough to understand they knew almost nothing yet about the job in front of them.

Franz spoke up. "When is the activity to take place, Carlos? I need to be sure my team is ready at the appropriate time."

"Good question," Carlos said. "We'll act on *Bastille* Day, July the 14th. Just three more days from now, in the morning. Franz, your team will start at 9:00 A.M. and finish by 10:00—just one hour."

Emile asked, "When will my team start?"

"At 10:15, and you will be finished by 11:15," Carlos answered.

Francois, listening to the others, commented, "Then I

---

5. Good, then.

suppose my team will start at 11:30 and finish at 12:30. Right, Carlos?"

"The twelve of you will only have to be busy for fifteen minutes each. For that, I'm paying each of you 1,500 Euros. That's 100 Euros per minute, so you can see why I'm expecting nothing less than perfection."

Again, Francois asked, "When do we find out what our jobs are to be? And where do we get the materials we'll need to do those jobs?"

"The four of us will meet at the entrance to the *Parc Champ de Mars*[6] on the Avenue Joseph Bouvard at 3:00 P.M. on July 13, the day before our job. There in the open and away from hidden microphones and spies, I will tell each of you separately exactly what you and your teams are to do. Each of you will know only the jobs of your team and not what the others will be doing. It's not necessary for anyone but me, Carlos the puma, to understand the grand design."

Carlos continued, "Then each of you will report here to my suite at half-hour intervals beginning at 6:00 P.M.— Franz at 6:00, Francois at 6:30, and Emile at 7:00—to receive the materials the members of your team will need. We will have no further contact after Emile leaves this suite. You have never heard of Carlos the puma, but you have visited a diamond salesman from South Africa in this suite to discuss the quality of the gems from his last shipment to your client, the Gem Exchange of Paris. Is that clear?"

Francois spoke, "Next time, Mr. Diamond Salesman,

---

6. Champ de Mars Park

there'd better not be any flawed gems, none, in our shipment. Am I being clear?"

Carlos smiled. "Excellent. That's the idea, Francois. Now I must call the front desk to retrieve some funds to pay you and your associates. Continue snacking."

Carlos picked up the phone and called the concierge. "This is the diamond salesman in your Charles de Gaulle suite. Could you please have a bellman bring me my sample case from the hotel safe? And then, if you will, check on the score of the cricket match between Islamabad and Abu Dhabi and come up in about 20 minutes to report that score to me. *Merci, Monsieur Concierge.*"[7]

As the three Gypsies continued eating and drinking, Carlos spoke to them once again. "When the concierge arrives with my sample case, you will all go into the bathroom and wait until I call you. There are things in that case that don't concern you."

✳ ✳ ✳

At the Offices of the French Intelligence Service

René had asked Luigi, Luisa and Cincinnati to go with him to the Intelligence Service for a 10:00 A.M. meeting with *Remy Dewclaux.* The head of Intelligence had texted him that he had a preliminary list of rich visitors to Paris over the past week.

"*Alors, Remy, qu'est-ce que tu as pour nous?*"[8] *René* asked

---

7. "Thank you, Mr. Concierge."
8. "So, Remy, what do you have for us?"

after introducing his twin cousins from Texas and the dancing pig from Ohio.

"From passport records, *René*, we have found that a few more than 11,000 foreign visitors passed through immigration in Paris in the last four days. We ran those names and passport numbers through our database and have found only one billionaire and six more whose net worth exceeds 50,000,000 Euros.

Perhaps your target is among these. If not, we can run a list of those worth more than 25,000,000 Euros."

Remy handed his visitors a computer print-out with a hand-written list attached. "Here is the list so far," Look at my hand-written list first. I did a little screening when I put it together."

Cincinnati and René spread the print-out on a table and placed *Remy*'s smaller list on top. Luigi and Luisa both scampered up onto the tabletop so they could see the lists, too.

Remy Dewclaux

Billionaires

Cecil Ratliff, M.P. —— England

Millionaires

Lady P. Du Pont —— England
Sheik A. Abdulla —— Saudi Arabia
Count F. Von Stuffel —— Hungary
A. Rodriguez —— USA
Ruth Steinmetz —— Israel
Eduard Moshe —— Russia

FIS French Intelligence Service

"What do we know about these individuals, *Remy?*" Cincinnati asked, looking at the shorter list.

"Sir Cecil and Lady Du Pont often travel together. He visits Paris at least three times a month on business, and Lady Du Pont occasionally accompanies him. They are an elderly couple and appear quite harmless.

"Sheik Abdulla represents his country in OPEC, and visits often to trade in European oil futures. He has never raised an eyebrow around here—in many years of visiting.

"Ruth Steinmetz, well, how shall I put this? She is one of us. We know her well and work with her secretly. Of course, that's not her real name." *Remy* looked uncomfortable discussing the Israeli visitor.

Cincinnati turned to the twins and said but one word, "Mossad."

Remy continued, "Visitors Rodriguez from the U.S. and Moshe from Russia are both members of a United Nations Conference on world health. Both are physicians—specialists in water purification and desert food crops."

"That leaves Count von Stuffel," *René* said. "That name seems very familiar to me. As if I had met him before or had some kind of dealings with him. Can you refresh my memory, *Remy?*"

"I'm not surprised you recall the name," Cincinnati interrupted. "He's been on our radar for some time."

Remy added, "Arrested several times—six, to be exact— in France. Four arrests in Paris for inciting riots and suspected sedition. Frankly, we think he's a wacko. Not quite right in the head. What is the C.I.A.'s interest in him, Cincinnati?"

"He claims to be a descendant of Emperor Franz Joseph. It's possible, although we haven't been able to trace his ancestry back directly. Frankly, we think he's a wacko, too. But he's never done anything we could pin on him directly. He always seems to want to hide in the shadows and pay someone else to do his illegal work for him."

"Bingo!" Luigi shouted. "He's suspect number one on my list of Carlos' possible employers."

Luisa joined in. "Does anybody have any idea what he might want Carlos to do here in Paris? Why would he hire Carlos the puma? Whatever it is, it must be big. And expensive. Carlos doesn't fool with small-time jobs."

"Right, Luisa," Cincinnati said. "I doubt if Carlos would return a phone call unless it promised at least two or three million Euros in payout."

"Of course, I remember him now," *René* said, smiling. "*Guy* and I had to chase him down one night outside of *Notre Dame*. He was trying to get a crowd of tourists to rush in and disrupt what he called a 'Pagan French Service.' That must have been one of his local arrests—about three years ago."

Luigi perked up and turned to *René*. "That means he's met *Guy Gondeaux*, and *Guy* has met him. At least they're not complete strangers. Good!"

Luisa, Cincinnati and *René* smiled at Luigi's comment, but *Remy* looked puzzled. He asked, "Why is that good— that your somewhat stupid assistant has met this Count von Stuffel? Is there some advantage in that?"

Cincinnati caught *René*'s attention and gave him a little frown and a slight "no" head shake.

René got the message. "It always helps to have had personal contact before with a suspect," he said to the head of French Intelligence. "And I, too, have some first-hand knowledge of this count."

"For now, at least, we'll concentrate on von Stuffel," Luigi said, adding to *Remy*, "but you will continue watching for really rich visitors, won't you? In case von Stuffel's not our guy?"

Cincinnati asked, "When he came through Immigration, was he asked where he would be staying while he was in Paris?"

"I can find that out," *Remy Dewclaux* said, "but we do know he maintains an apartment in Paris. On the *Champs Elysée*,[10] right at the head of the street in the second building from the *Arc de Triomphe*[11] next door to the Publicis world headquarters."

"What's a Publicis?" Luisa wanted to know.

"It's a huge advertising agency with offices all over the world," *René* answered. "It was started about seventy years ago by the best friend of Charles de Gaulle."

"Did he have a gigantic nose?" Luigi blurted out.

Luisa almost fell off the table in a fit of laughter.

René and Cincinnati also burst out laughing, leaving *Remy* wondering if they had all gone bonkers at once.

"We all know the general's nose was quite large," *René* answered. "As to his friend's, I don't know, Luigi. Maybe when we finish off Carlos, we can make an inquiry, no?"

---

10. The Champs Elysee is the main shopping boulevard in Paris. Many expensive shops and company headquarters are on it.
11. A monument to one of Napoleon I's war victories.

As *René*, Cincinnati and the kittens left the office, Cincinnati said to the twins, "Looks like your plan is right on. Congratulations."

Luisa answered, "That is, assuming *Guy Gondeaux* isn't really totally stupid and will do what *René* tells him."

Once they were off the elevator and out on the street, Luigi had something to say. "For some reason, I just don't feel good about that guy *Remy*. *René*, do you think we can really trust him?"

"You're very astute, Luigi. My answer is I just don't know."

* * *

Back at the Charles de Gaulle Suite in the Paris Ritz Hotel

At a sharp rap on the door, Emile, Francois and Franz hurried into the bathroom, careful to take the tray of snacks with them. They seemed determined to make every crumb disappear before they had to leave Carlos' suite.

Carlos opened the door to the concierge, asking him to *attendre juste en moment*[12] while Carlos got some money out of the sample case to pay the Gypsies their first one-third share of the cash they were earning for doing whatever it was Carlos wanted them to do on *Bastille* Day.

Carlos carefully counted out twelve 500 Euro notes, handed the concierge a 20 Euro bill and the sample case and said, "Please come back as soon as you return this sample case to the hotel safe. I'll then require the score of the cricket match, and you'll be able to lead these scruffy

---

12. wait just a minute

guests down the service elevator and out the back door, no?"

"*Merci, Monsieur,*"[13] the concierge said as he picked up the sample case and headed for the elevators. Little did he know the case contained not diamond samples, but an arsenal of smoke bombs and C-4 plastic explosives.

Carlos let the three Gypsies stay in the bathroom. He really didn't want to watch them eat the goodies he'd ordered. *Such pigs they are,* he thought. *And petty criminals. They'll do this job for a pittance while Carlos will get five million Euros. Ah, but that's why they will forever be poor Gypsies and Carlos will be Carlos, the best of the best. And very, very rich.*

✳ ✳ ✳

Back in the Office of Remy Dewclaux, Head of French Intelligence

Remy reached for his secure phone and flipped off the switch that controlled the automatic recording device for the line.

There will be no recording of this call.

His number dialed and an answer received, he spoke softly into the handset. "Von Stuffel, there may be problems. When does your agent arrive?"

Uh, oh. Do you think Luigi was right about Remy? *Can he be trusted? Will the Gypsies take their one-third payment and run? Or will they meet with Carlos and follow through with his plan? And exactly what is his plan? Why does he need twelve Gypsies each to do something fifteen minutes apart? Do you think Luigi and Luisa will ever tell Dusty what really happened to her new hat?*

---

13. "Thank you, Sir."

Parlez Vous Francais?
by Luigi and Luisa

We're not Cincinnati this time. He said we could write one vocabulary list for you. By now you must know we love ice cream . . . Mmmmm. If you do, too, we wanted you to be able to order your favorite flavor in French. So here are a number of flavors. *Bon Appetit!* [14]

English	French	Say It Like This
vanilla	*vanille*	vah-NEE-yeh
chocolate	*chocolat*	sho-coh-LAH
strawberry	*fraise*	FREHZ
peach	*péche*	PESZH
raspberry	*frambroise*	frahm-BWAHS
banana	*banana*	bah-NAH-nah
pistachio	*pistache*	peesz-TOSH
caramel	*caramel*	cah-rah-MEHL
hazelnut	*noisette*	nwah-SZEHT
cherry	*cerise*	sair-EEZ
sardine (Luigi's favorite)	*sardine*	sahr-DEEN

---

14. Good appetite!

* Chapter 14 *
Guy commence son travail et Carlos decide sa fuite[1]

Brigade Criminelle Headquarters—René's Office

Luisa and Luigi had been talking to *Guy Gondeaux* for almost an hour while *René*, Dusty, Buzzer and Cincinnati worked at their computers trying to find out more about Count Freidrich von Stuffel.

"This von Stuffel's a real piece of work," Cincinnati said. "His father owned armament factories that used slave labor during the big war, and so he became very, very rich. He left all his money and his businesses to his son, this Freidrich character. Looks like Freidrich sold the businesses and stashed the cash—maybe as much as ten billion Euros. He lives in high style from the earnings of his accounts. And he uses them to finance his activities, one of which seems to be, somehow, to get even with the French, or, more specifically, the Parisians."

---

1. *Guy Goes to Work, and Carlos Plans His Escape*

"How much is ten billion Euros?" Dusty asked. "In real money?"

René laughed. "And you Americans call the French 'parochial,' Dusty. Ten billion Euros today would be about 14 or 15 billion U.S. dollars—in real money, as you call it."

Buzzer smiled at an embarrassed Dusty Louise to let her know what she had said was okay, particularly since they were all family. Then he asked Cincinnati and *René*, "Do we have any idea why the count would want to get even with the people of Paris?"

René typed a few strokes into his computer, looked at the screen and then at Buzzer. "According to his arrest records here in Paris, he seems to be trying to avenge a slight or defeat suffered by one of his ancestors, perhaps even Franz Joseph, himself. In his file at *Prefecture de Police*[2] he was ranting about 'righting wrongs' of long ago several times when we arrested him. I seem to remember that, on the night *Guy* and I picked him up, he kept babbling in Hungarian about something bad having happened more than a hundred years ago. And he repeated that it was his destiny to avenge whatever it was he thought so terrible. But, alas, my knowledge of Hungarian is limited mostly to 'goulash' and a few other tasty foods. *Guy*, of course, barely speaks coherent French. I can tell you, though, that the count was entirely agitated. He was very upset about something."

"Do you have a historian in the *Brigade Criminelle*, *René?*" Cincinnati asked. "Someone who could do a bit of quick backtracking to see what event involving Emperor Franz

---

2. Police Department

Joseph and the City of Paris might have happened, probably sometime in the last half of the nineteenth century?"

"Indeed I have just such an expert, actually. *Le capitain du quatrième command*[3] earned her degree in French history at the *Sorbonne*.[4] She will be familiar with the time period, and I'm sure—if this count isn't just a complete, how would you say, nut?—she will either know or be able to find the answer quickly." *René* seemed almost excited. "I'll call her right now if the three of you will check to see how the twins are getting on with *Guy*."

René reached for his phone as Buzzer, Cincinnati and Dusty turned to go into the room next door where Luigi and Luisa were coaching *Guy* on his new role and responsibilities.

✱ ✱ ✱

Later the Same Evening in the Bar Vendôme in the Paris Ritz Hotel

Carlos, still disguised as a diamond salesman from South Africa, sat at a corner table with his two pilots, *Jacques* and *Georges*.

"When will you need us again?" *Jacques* asked the big puma.

"Not soon, *Jacques*," Carlos replied. "Today is July 11. My work here will take place on the morning of July 14, *Bastille* Day. For the next two days I'll rest and complete my plan, and I'll commit it to memory."

---

3. the captain of my fourth command
4. The Sorbonne is a famous university in Paris.

Never write anything down, he thought.

"On the morning of *Bastille* Day, when all of Paris will be on the streets celebrating, I'll be up early. And I'll be through with my job here by early afternoon, right after lunch," Carlos continued. "The sky will be full of fireworks and hot air balloons and kite flyers."

"So you'll want to leave in the Gulfstream by mid-afternoon?" *Georges* asked. "And where will we be going? Back to Argentina?"

"No, not so quickly, *Georges*," Carlos said as he took another sip of his Coca-Cola Zero. "You and *Jacques allez partir avec l'avion. Sans moi.*[5]

"My departure from Paris cannot be so public as a private airplane from a major airport," Carlos went on, munching on a bowl of olives that had been set on their small round table. "You'll file a flight plan to Milan in Italy, but change it in-flight to Munich in Bavaria. I'll meet you there late that same night, at the Holiday Inn downtown— the one near the *grand station de train*.[6] Our rooms there are already reserved. So you'll know, I'll be a salesman of fine caviar from Russia."

"May I ask, Carlos, how you will get from Paris to Munich? And why would we stay at such a *bourgeois*[7] place as a Holiday Inn? You always stay at the best of the best, no?" *Jacques* asked.

Carlos smiled, but shook a paw at his pilots in a minor scolding. He said, "Carlos does not consider class as impor-

---

5. will leave with the plane that morning. Without me.
6. big train station
7. Bourgeois is a French word used in many languages to denote 'middle class'

tant, *Gentilhommes*.[8] Don't get spoiled to the life of the rich and infamous just because you're Carlos' chosen pilots. Remember, I'm rich because of what I do. And how well I do it. But half the population of the world lives in relative poverty. In fact 99-plus percent live less well than Carlos."

He smiled and looked around the room. Then he went on, "Does that make them lesser creatures? I think not. Perhaps they aren't able to do what Carlos does. Maybe they wouldn't if they could. So I'm grateful there's room for me at the top. But never look down on a lesser hotel, especially one as good as the Holiday Inn in downtown Munich."

The two pilots looked sheepish, just as Carlos intended.

Then the big puma laughed a hearty laugh and said, "The real reason for the Holiday Inn is that I'll be arriving late at night—perhaps after midnight. Also, it's close to the train station, and good enough for a few short nights."

Georges felt relieved enough by now to ask another question. "Will you take the train from Paris to Munich?"

"Only the last part of the trip will be by train," Carlos said. "Did you remember to bring the kit flyer with us? The one with the sky-blue wing canopy?"

"You're not going to fly that thing from Paris, are you Carlos?" *Jacques* looked distressed. "It's little more than a kite with a small motor. Very dangerous."

Carlos shook his head slowly. "There are certain dangers for everyone every day. The owl eats a mouse, and the mouse has a bad day, even though he did nothing to deserve

---

8. Gentlemen

it. A condor then eats the owl. Is that the owl's fault? And then a reckless human with little or no brain shoots the condor out of the sky with a gun and has it stuffed to rest on his fireplace's mantel. Has the condor been careless? We can only hope that the human with the gun gets run down by a bus the next day, no?"

He went on. "What I'm telling you is there are always risks. In Carlos' work, some risks are bigger than most. But you know that I'm extremely careful when I work. I'm never hungry, and I'm always rested. Everything is planned to perfection. If something goes wrong—and it almost never does—we have to be flexible. And always have a backup plan ready. Just in case.

"So, yes, my friends, Carlos will be one of you pilots from Paris to *Mont Blanc*.[9] From there, I'll abandon the flying kite, as you call it, and let Eurail take me on to Turin and Munich."

Jacques, resigned to trusting Carlos, said, "Where do you want us to leave the aircraft, then?"

When Carlos told them where to leave the little collapsible plane, along with an extra five-gallon can of gasoline on the night of July 13, both the pilots smiled.

Carlos is not a fool. I will have no problem taking off from there and clearing the city in mere minutes amongst the hot air balloons, fireworks, and the other kites.

* * *

---

9. Mont Blanc is a famous mountain on the French-Italian-Swiss border. In Italian, it's called *Monte Bianco*. Both names mean 'white mountain.'

Back at René's Office at the Brigade Criminelle

As they approached the room next door to *René's* office, Dusty, Buzzer, Cincinnati and *René* heard loud laughter. Luigi and Luisa were rolling on the floor, holding their sides as they laughed hysterically. *Guy* was jumping up and down, snortling in his own peculiar way.

Dusty jumped to her own conclusion. "What in Sam Hill is going on in here!" she demanded, as the twins tried, without much success, to stifle their laughter. "You two are supposed to be coaching *Guy*, here, on his new job of getting close to Count von Stuffel. Instead I find all of you *riant comme des hyènas,*[10] rolling in the floor and, quite obviously, playing instead of working!" Dusty was her usual indignant self, but was shocked that she actually spoke to the twins in French.

Getting his laughter under control, Luigi tried his normal trick of changing the subject. "Who is Sam Hill, Dusty?" he asked. That question set Luisa and *Guy* into another round of laughter.

Buzzer said, "Let them calm down a minute, Dusty, and then I'm sure they'll tell us how their laughter related to their work."

"After all, Cincinnati put in, "Work doesn't all have to be all serious, does it?"

René smiled. "*Certainement non. Travail doit être quelques fois agreable aussi.*"[11]

"After all, Cincinnati added, "work doesn't all have to be serious, does it?"

---

10. laughing like hyenas
11. "Certainly not. Work should sometimes be fun, too."

Dusty wasn't convinced, but she knew better than to argue with Buzzer. Still, she didn't appreciate that *René* and Cincinnati were ganging up on her.

When the twins had calmed down to snickering, and *Guy* returned to his glassy-eyed expression, Buzzer spoke up again. "Okay, Luigi and Luisa, would one of you please tell us what you've accomplished here in the last hour?"

Luigi looked at his sister, who nodded that he should go ahead and speak.

"*Guy* is ready, absolutely," Luigi said. "We've helped him come up with a brilliant disguise guaranteed to fool not only Count von Stuffel, but also every one of you."

"He looks the same to me." Dusty said, still disapproving.

"Wait 'til you see this," Luisa said. "Ready, *Guy*?" she asked.

Guy nodded, and Luisa began to speak to him in her gravelly Ma Kettle voice. "I see you've been learnin' how to fergit yer fancy Frenchiness, there, Pa," she said.

Guy slumped his shoulders and screwed up his face. He spoke English in a high-pitched monotone voice. "Shurr 'nuff, Ma. I shed all my Frenchie ways, an' now I'm as common as salt and as rich as the Beverly Hillbillies."

Luigi said in his normal kitten voice. "Tell them who you are now."

"I'm Gary Gonzachu from up near Syracuse, New York, an' I'm here in France on a special trip 'at has ta do with m' bizness."

"And what's yer bizness, Pa?" Luisa asked.

"I'm a egg farmer. Got me near to 90,000 hens inna great huge barn just a'laying them eggs ta beat Billy. Purt near two-and-a-half million dozen last year alone. That's a lotta eggs, ya know?"

"And why are you in France, Pa?" Luigi asked.

"Cause ya just gets tired a scrambled and sunny-side up and fried hard. I aim ta hire me a Frenchie chef ta show me how ta make them fancy Frenchie dishes with eggs. Stuff like *omelets et crêpes et quiches*.[12] Anythin' fancy an' cont'nental soundin' 'at uses up a lotta eggs."

"Well, Pa," Luisa went on as Ma Kettle, "How's 'at gonna help ya git close ta the Count von Stuffel? Duz he care a whole bunch 'bout eggs? Or layers?"

Guy, aka Gary Gonzachu, answered, "Don't reckin he duz, Ma. But see, I'm a Hungarian, too. Yep, went over to the U.S. of A. 'bout fifteen years ago. I'm the first cousin the count's never met. Got me *bona fide*[13] identee'fications, I do. We're gonna be real glad to see one another fer the first time ever. When's I knock on his door an' interduces m'self."

René was dumbstruck. *Who is this cat, anyway? He looks like Guy, but he can't possibly be.* He asked Luigi and Luisa, "What have you done with my assistant? Where is *Guy Gondeaux*?"

---

12. Omelets and crepes and quiches are all French words we use regularly in English.
13. Authentic. In Latin and English, *bona fide*.

Luisa smiled and dropped her Ma Kettle act. "You're looking at him, cousin. We told you *Guy* was smarter than you think. Know what? He speaks French and English and Hungarian. So he's perfect as the long-lost cousin of the Count von Stuffel and a direct descendant of the great Franz Joseph."

Luigi added, "Of course, he's not Hungarian. And he's never been to New York. We just made that part up."

Buzzer and Cincinnati applauded softly. Once again, Dusty was embarrassed at having misjudged and underestimated the cleverness of the twins.

But *René* still seemed to doubt what he was seeing. He spoke to *Guy*, "What is it you will do as this long-lost Hungarian cousin to help us all catch Carlos?"

Guy stared at his boss. "I am to quickly get close to the count, claim to be the rich American farmer from New York who came there from Hungary—his long-lost cousin who has been quite unhappy with the French since my grandfather told me stories about them when I was a child. That way, I can not only find out what his problem is with Parisians, but also I can learn what he's hired Carlos to do, before it happens. So we can stop it in time."

René turned to Luigi and Luisa. "I was told you two were clever, but *sacre bleu*,[14] you are much more than simply clever. You are miracle workers. One hour with *Guy Gondeau* and you've turned a *mannequin*[15] into a clever secret agent. *Mon Dieu, c'est un miracle!*"[16]

---

14. A French exclamation. Literally, it means 'blue blood.'
15. A dummy or inanimate model. Another French word we use in English.
16. "My God, it's a miracle!"

Cincinnati said. *"René,* this is a typical piece of work from these two little scamps. You may wish to hire them in the future, but you'll have to compete for their services with the *Policía Federal de Argentina,* the *Federales* in Mexico, the Italian *Carabiniere* and, of course, our own Cats In Action. All of them have seen the results of their work, and all are as surprised and pleased as you are."

Do you think Carlos will be able to take off from his target in a motor-powered kite? And where is his target, anyway? What little conflict in history do you think has the count so bent out of shape? Or is he just a nut? Will Guy be able to fool the count as this secret agent named Gary Gonzachu? And how did Luigi and Luisa turn the seemingly stupid Guy into such a clever actor in just one hour? Or is the new Guy really somebody else?

Parlez Vous Francais?

by Cincinnati

The twins have taught you the names of many flavors of ice cream. *Bien!*[17] Now let's learn how to say *les noms de certains sports.*[18]

English	French	Say It Like This
baseball	*base-ball*	BAYSZ-bahl
basketball	*basket-ball*	BAHS-ket-bahl
cycling	*aller en bicyclette*	ahl-LEH OH(n) bee-see-CLEHT
auto racing	*course aux autos*	COHR-sah au zah-toh
skiing	*faire du ski*	fare deu SKEE
football	*le football*	leh FUHT-bahl
gymnastics	*gymnastique*	jim-sahs-TEEK
hockey	*hockey*	OH-kay
running	*courrir*	coor-EER
sailing	*faire de la voile*	fare-deh lah VWAHL
soccer	*jouer au ballon*	zhoo-air oh bahl-LOH(n)
swimming	*natation*	nah-tah-SZYOH(n)
tennis	*tennis*	ten-NEES
volleyball	*volleyball*	VOHL-ee-bohl
golf	*golf*	GOLF

---

17. Good
18. the names of some sports

* Chapter 15 *
Guy rencontre le Comte, et l'énigme se clarifie[1]

In the Offices of Remy Dewclaux, Head of the French Intelligence Bureau
After switching on the white-noise machine to make the conversation in his office secure from eavesdropping devices, *Remy* looked across his desk to the Count von Stuffel, who sat quietly, and relaxed.

Remy said, "I have told you, Count, that the American cats and their pig friend from the secret American Cats In Action are working with the *Brigade Criminelle*. They're after Carlos the puma, the infamous terrorist from Argentina. In their search for him, your name has surfaced—along with others. So you should be careful."

"Thank you, *Remy*," Count von Stuffel said. "Yes, I am aware of this Carlos and, perhaps, may have dealings with him. But I will be careful not to do anything wrong, myself."

---

1. Guy Meets the Count, and a Puzzle Comes Together

"Good. Just watch out. We can't risk the master plan at this early stage. There is far too much to gain for both of us to get caught up in some paranoid foolishness." *Remy* stopped, realizing he was lecturing the count. He still wasn't comfortable the count wasn't up to something really stupid.

"Tell me, Freidrich," *Remy* insisted, "tell me that you're not trying some dumb thing about getting even with the people of Paris, again. That would set us back years, if not forever. You're not involved, are you, with this terrorist Carlos?"

"Please do not be concerned, *Remy*. You have your business, I have my business, and we have our joint business. The three are not connected.

The count rose to leave. "I must go, now," the count said, thinking, *to meet with this Carlos at the Paris Ritz. To find out how he's planning to blow up the monument to that ridiculous French 'victory.' And see if he's really a cat like he claims to be.*

* * *

Back at The Suite at the Georges Cinq Hotel

Luigi and Luisa hadn't wanted to come back to the hotel when they all left *René*'s office, but Dusty had insisted the two of them needed to take a nap.

"After all," she said, "you two must have been awake half the night conjuring up that plan to turn *Guy* into a double agent."

"No!" came the answer in unison from the twins.

Luigi said, "We can think fast, and work fast. It didn't take us all that long."

"Some of us are just quicker than others," Luisa said, instantly realizing she'd probably insulted Dusty yet once again.

Buzzer spoke up to save the twins from their big sister's wrath. "Before you two take a nap, Cincinnati and I want you to call Dr. Buford and Bogart-BOGART back at the ranch in the Hill Country. I promised to call them when we were sure Carlos had made it to Paris. He must be here by now, probably resting at some posh hotel.

"Call them and tell them what's happening," he said as he handed Luigi his satellite phone. "Here, use this one with the scrambler—not the hotel phone. Who knows if it might be bugged?"

Uh-oh, Buzzer thought, *I just said 'who knows.'*

Sure enough, Luigi and Luisa snickered, put their paws in front of their mouths to try to stifle a belly laugh, and then lost it, rolling in the floor. They kept repeating "nose," and they just couldn't stop.

✳ ✳ ✳

In René's Offices at the Brigade Criminelle

Guy Gondeaux, a.k.a. Gary Gonzachu, New York egg producer, had received his training and his basic marching orders from Luigi and Luisa. He was ready to go into action as a double agent. His job would be to win the confidence of Count Freidrich von Stuffel, his fake long-lost cousin, in order to find out what Carlos was doing in Paris and, with a little luck, maybe help short-circuit Carlos' plan.

But his everyday boss, *René Francois Fopaux*, the new head of the *Brigade Criminelle*, still had his doubts, both about Guy's transformation from village idiot to super-smart sleuth . . . and about his ability to carry off the assignment secretly and successfully.

René wanted tactical details. He wanted to know exactly how *Guy* would go about his project. And *René* was becoming frustrated because *Guy* wasn't giving out the specific details.

"*Dis moi une fois de plus, Guy,*[2] how it is you're going to approach the count?" *René* asked.

"*Je vais simplement frapper a la porte de son appartement,*[3] introduce myself as his long-lost first cousin in Hungary, now an egg farmer in New York, and invite him to a brunch tomorrow morning. I'll tell him I've hired a famous chef to prepare a variety of egg dishes for us to sample while we become reacquainted.

"*Cela n'est pas difficile, René,*"[4] Guy insisted. "Then I will have to, as Luigi and Luisa said, 'play it by ear.' *Ne vous inquiétez pas, Monsieur,*[5] as the American kittens said, '*Guy* is not as stupid as he seems.' I'll get the straight story. And if he tries to hold out on me, I have my methods for extracting information."

René looked shocked. "I've never heard you speak so many sentences at one time, *Guy*, certainly not so many that actually made sense. What's happened to you?"

"A half-hour with your little cousins has changed my life. They convinced me I could become the next Sherlock

---

2. "Tell me again, Guy
3. "I'll simply knock on his apartment door
4. "It's not difficult, René,"
5. "Don't worry, Sir,

Holmes—that I didn't forever have to be Inspector *Clouseau.* They told me about a senator in their country who says to himself every morning, 'I'm good enough; I'm smart enough; and, doggone it, people like me.' Maybe I, too, will become a senator some day," *Guy* said.

"But in the meantime, Sir, we have to stop Carlos the puma. And I'm going to get the information from that crazy count to do just that."

"When will you start?" *René* asked.

"Just as soon as Luigi and Luisa wake up from their nap. The three of us are going to see Count Freidrich von Stuffel together. They'll be my children, Nick and Nikki, twins on holiday from their studies at Oxford."

"You will keep me informed, won't you, *Guy?*" *René* asked. "Same as always in the old days when you were merely an idiot?"

"Of course, *Monsieur,* but this time Luigi will be my mouthpiece, and Luisa will be our moll."

"Whatever do you mean by that, *Guy?*" *René* asked, growing more and more baffled by the change in his assistant.

Guy replied, *"Je n'ai pas d'idée, Monsieur,*[6] but that's what Luigi and Luisa said to explain our roles. Something to do with American movies, criminals and Jimmy Cagney."

✶ ✶ ✶

Back at the Suite at the Georges Cinq Hotel
Luisa, using Buzzer's satellite phone with its scrambler,

---

6. "I have no idea, Sir"

dialed their ranch back in the Texas Hill Country. After two rings, Bogart-BOGART answered, *"Allò. Ici c'est le chien intelligent au ranch de Buzzer au Texas.*[7] To whom am I speaking, *S'il vous plait?"*[8]

"It's Luisa, Bogart-BOGART. We're in Paris in a really swanky hotel. But we're pretending to be British royalty, twins Nick and Nikki on holiday from our studies at Oxford. How're things back in Texas? It seems like an age since we've been home."

"Well, Luisa, it has been more than a week. And Dr. Buford and I miss all of you. What time is it there in Paris, anyway?"

"It's 2:00 in the afternoon here, so it must be only about 7:00 in the morning there. I didn't wake you and Dr. Buford up, did I?"

"Certainement pas,"[9] the big dog answered. "You know how it is here . . . Early to bed, and early to rise—gives us all bloodshot, teary red eyes. Did you notice I'm speaking some French?"

"Oui, j'ai remarqué,"[10] and we're proud of you for that. Bogart-BOGART, Luigi wants to fill you and Dr. Buford in on what's happening here. Can you both listen on the speakerphone?"

"Oui, Luisa, juste un moment, s'il te plait,"[11] Bogart-BOGART answered as Luisa handed the little satellite phone to Luigi.

---

7. "Hello, this is the smart dog at Buzzer's ranch in Texas."
8. please
9. "Of course not"
10. "Yes, I did."
11. "Yes, Luisa, just a minute, please."

"Hello, Bogart-BOGART and Dr. Buford Lewis. Luigi here with an update on our caper."

"*Comment cela procede?*"[12] Dr. Buford asked as he joined the conversation.

"Well, we all got here early yesterday and spent some time looking over the city. We saw the *Eiffel Tower* in the daytime and again at night with about a bazillion lights on it. And we went to the Left Bank, which you might already know is right across from the Right Bank. In the sewers, we saw some rats as big as hippopotamuses, but Luisa and I scared them away."

"*Il semble amusant,*[13] Luigi, but what about Carlos? Is he there yet?" Dr. Buford tried to turn the conversation from sightseeing to crime-fighting.

"We're sure he's here. He should have arrived this morning. He was about a day behind us. Did you hear about the French Foreign Legion Barracks in Casablanca? Now we know why he stopped in Marrakech—to blow something up, of course," Luigi continued.

"Get to the point, Luigi," Luisa said. "You're just rambling, *petit frère.*"[14]

Luigi gave a quick recap of the plan he and Luisa had come up with during the night, and reported on the amazing change in *Guy Gondeaux,* whom they'd turned into a street-smart, secret double-agent.

"That's where we are at the moment, Dr. Buford and Bogart-BOGART," Luigi summed up. "Dusty says we have

---

12. "How's it going?"
13. "Sounds like fun."
14. little brother

to take a nap now before we get with the new and improved *Guy* to go see this count nut."

Dr. Buford said quickly, "*C'est ridicule.*[15] You two are major-league detectives leading the charge. If you're not sleepy, why take a nap? Let me talk to Dusty Louise. I'll have a few words with her, and you'll be ready to go back to work right away."

Luigi and Luisa shrugged, and Luisa called, "Dusty, Dr. Buford wants to talk to you!"

As Dusty took the phone from Luigi, Luisa whispered to her brother, "Let's get in bed real quick and pretend to take a nap. That way, the evil queen won't think we put Dr. Buford up to helping us skip a nap."

Luigi looked puzzled. "We didn't, did we?"

"*Non,*"[16] Luisa said, "but that's what she'll think. Trust me. Pretend you're snoring. Quick!"

With that, the twins slipped into bed, slammed their eyes shut and began snoring with a sound that resembled a couple of bumblebees circling a flower garden.

Dusty put down the phone and said in a loud voice, "Get up, you two. You have important work to do."

"You mean we don't get to take a little nap?" Luigi asked, looking disappointed.

Luisa piped up, "Actually, I'm not really sleepy, Luigi. Let's call *Guy* and get on with our mission."

* * *

---

15. "That's ridiculous."
16. "No"

In Carlos' Charles de Gaulle Suite at the Paris Ritz

Between the phone call from the Count von Stuffel and Carlos' meeting with him in the Hemingway Bar, the big puma pulled out a map of Paris and began to study the exact locations of a list of a dozen monuments and historic locations he'd first memorized on the flight from Brazil to Marrakech. He was tempted to mark the locations on the map. But he'd learned long ago that in his line of work, leaving written evidence around was not smart.

Instead, he simply wrote the names and addresses of the twelve on separate slips of paper and clipped them together in groups of four locations each. And the four locations in each of the three sets had to be in order and close together. The first group was all south of the Seine and numbered one through four from south to north. The second group took up where the first group ended and proceeded more or less farther south to north as well. The third group continued north until it was quite near the real target—the target he would personally deal with, and fly away from.

When he was finished sorting the twelve slips into three groups, he wrote a name on each group: *Emile, Franz* and *Francois*.

His mapping and sorting complete, he put all the slips into an envelope which he slipped into the small safe in his bathroom. Typical of his cautious approach, he also put into the safe a small ball of C-4 plastic explosives with an electronic detonator that he could trigger from as far away as five kilometers. If he needed to do away with any potentially damaging evidence, of course.

Then he lay down to wait for his wake-up call for his

meeting with the count—the count who was becoming much too curious for Carlos. When they met, he would remind the count that "curiosity killed the cat," but cats have at least seven, maybe nine lives. Counts only have one. And so, I can make this count dance to my tune with a not-so-gentle reminder.

What do you suppose is the business that the count and Remy Dewclaux *have in common? Will the twins get into trouble with Dusty because Dr. Buford Lewis told her not to make them take a nap? Is Guy still mostly an idiot? Or has he become a seriously smart, secret double-agent? And what do you think will happen when Luigi and Luisa and* Guy *go to see the count? Will he fall for their tricks?*

Parlez Vous Français?

by Cincinnati

Comment vous dite votre nom en français?[17] Here are some names in English and the way you would say them in French.

English	French	Say It Like This
Charles	Charles	SHARL
Christopher	Christopher	CRIS-toh-fehr
David	David	dah-VEED
Donald	Donald	doh-NAHLD
Edward	Édouard	ed-WAHRD
Frank	François	frah(n)-SWAH
George	Georges	ZHORZ
Henry	Henri	oh(n)-REE
Joseph	Joseph	JOH-sef
Joe	Joseph	JOH-sef
James	Jacques	SZAHK
Matthew	Mathias	mah-TEE-ehs
Peter	Pierre	pee-AIR
Robert	Robert	roh-BEHR
Thomas	Thomas	toh-MASZ
Luigi	Louis	loo-EE
William	Guillaume	gwee-OHM
Ann	Anne	AHN
Barbara	Barbara	BAHR-bahr-ah
Kathleen	Catherine	cah-TREEN
Deborah	Débora	DEH-bohr-ah
Elaine	Hélène	eh-LEHN

---

17. How do you say your name in French?

Guy rencontre le Comte, et l'énigme se clarifie

Frances	*France*	FRAHNZ
Elizabeth	*Elisabeth*	ehl-ees-ah-BEHT
Linda	*Linda*	LEEN-dah
Louise	*Louise*	loo-EESZ
Margaret	*Marguerite*	mahr-gahr-EET
Martha	*Marthe*	MAHR-teh
Mary	*Marie*	mah-REE
Rose	*Rosette*	roh-SZET
Sarah	*Sarah*	SAH-rah
Susan	*Suzanne*	soo-ZAHN
Sophia	*Sophie*	SOH-fee

Part Four

A Double Agent

Everybody thinks *Guy* is stupid—the village idiot. But we know better. With a little help from the two of us, he'll be able to get that nutty count to spill the beans. Then all we have to do is sit and wait for Carlos. He won't stand a chance.

—Luigi and Luisa
Just Doin' Our Jobs

* Chapter 16 *

Le plan se complique, et le comte parle[1]

Next Morning at the Café Madeleine—Breakfast
Guy and Luigi and Luisa had not been able to find Count von Stuffel at home the previous afternoon. Unknown to them, of course, he had been meeting with *Remy Dewclaux*, head of the French Intelligence Service and, later, with his hired terrorist, Carlos the puma.

They had, however, been able to reach him by phone later in the evening, and *Guy*, pretending to be his long-lost Hungarian cousin Gary Gonzachu, egg farmer from upstate New York, had invited him to breakfast, as planned. The count, excited at the chance to connect with a lost family member, accepted the invitation at once.

René had called his friend, the owner of the *Café Madeleine* on the *Champs Elysee*, and simply asked him to take special care of some guests the next morning for break-

---
1. The Plot Thickens, and the Count Talks

fast—three Americans. A prominent egg farmer and his twin children, Nick and Nikki. *René* explained the breakfast would be a family reunion of sorts and that the egg farmer wanted to sample a variety of breakfast foods containing eggs.

The café owner assured *René* the party of four would be treated as honored guests. *"Tous leurs désires seront mon plaisir,"*[2] he had said.

So when the double agent arrived with Luisa and Luigi, the restaurant's staff welcomed them with unusual courtesy, seating them at the very best table in front where they could see the traffic and pedestrians on the *Champs Elysee* through the big front windows.

The three "Americans" had just sat down when Count von Stuffel entered the café and walked up to their table.

Guy stood and said, "Ah, you must be my long-lost *cousin,*[3] the Count Freidrich von Stuffel. I'm so pleased to meet you at last. I, of course, am Gary Gonzachu from New York and originally from near Budapest, and these are my two children, Nick and Nikki. They're studying agricultural production at Oxford with an emphasis on hens and eggs.

"Thank you so much for joining us," *Guy* continued. "The chef has agreed this morning to serve us sample portions of several French egg dishes so that I can go back to the U.S.A. and include continental recipes in my cartons of eggs. To sell more of them, of course."

Smiling, the count nodded politely to each of them and

---

2. "Their every wish will be my pleasure."
3. cousin

said, "*Je suis allergique aux oeufs.*[4] Perhaps you won't be offended if I have instead some *lard et saucisse avec toast?*"[5]

Luisa said, "Thank you, Sir, but Nick and I are vegetabularians."

Luigi added, "We prefer not to eat our fellow creatures, but you certainly may have whatever you want. We'll stick to sampling eggs. And perhaps some chocolate cake and ice cream."

Guy went straight to business. "Tell us all about yourself, Count. We want to know all about our famous cousin in the old country. And what you're up to here in Paris."

Before the count could begin, a waiter walked up with a large tray covered with several kinds of egg dishes. "*S'il vous plait savourez,*"[6] he said as he set the dishes on the table.

Luigi said, "Our cousin, the famous count, would like some sausage, bacon and toast, please."

The waiter answered, "*Comme vous desirez, Monsieur,*"[7] and headed straight for the kitchen. Then the count began to tell his story.

* * *

In René's Office at the Brigade Criminelle

As Dusty, Cincinnati and Buzzer Louis walked into *René Fopaux*'s office while the kittens were at breakfast with the count and *Guy*, they found Buzzer's look-alike in the red beret on the phone and seeming pretty excited.

---

4. "I am allergic to eggs."
5. bacon and sausage with toast
6. "Please enjoy."
7. "As you wish, Sir."

"*Oui? Non. Vraiment? Bien!*"[8] he said at intervals into the phone he was holding in his left paw while gesturing with his right for them to come on in and have a seat. With a "Thank you, *Marlene*," he put down the phone.

Turning to his three American guests, *René* said, "We may have a lead on the motives of the crazy Hungarian, Count von Stuffel. I was just speaking with the *capitaine*[9] of my fourth company, the one who is a French historian, you remember? She told me a most interesting story, although it's not complete yet. She's still doing a bit of research at the *bibliothèque*[10] at the Sorbonne.

"But here's what she thinks so far," *René* said. "Sometime in the 1870s, the French army mistakenly attacked a small town on the Austrian border. Clearly they were lost, so they were unaware that they were attacking the wrong place. Mistake or not, though, they shouldn't have done what they did. Their actions so incensed Franz Joseph, the head of the Austro-Hungarian Empire, that he brought a large force to Paris, surrounding the town at night.

"He demanded an apology and payment for damages, but the French government didn't know what he was talking about, and so refused his demands. He laid siege to the

---

8. "Yes? No. Really? Good!"
9. captain
10. library

city, cutting off all the roads and the Seine. Nothing could be delivered into the city, and soon the people of Paris were facing starvation, and they even began eating rats from the sewers." He shook his head at the thought.

"Before anyone actually starved, however, Franz had his troops withdraw and return to Vienna and Budapest," *René* went on. "Somehow one of the officials in Paris must have decided to make an outrageous, though believable claim, and declared victory for France over Franz Joseph.

"There was friction for many years after that," *René* concluded. "My captain thinks perhaps this is what may still be upsetting the count."

Buzzer looked thoughtful. "Sometimes it takes nothing more significant than a slight that's more than a hundred years unresolved to set off fireworks in the brain of someone who is mentally unstable to begin with. But I don't see how this information brings us closer to any specific target the count may have hired Carlos to attack."

"When will we hear more from your captain?" Cincinnati asked. "The pieces of this puzzle are starting to come together, but we still won't know what picture it forms until we get a few more pieces in place."

"She's very reliable, this particular captain," *René* said. "And smart. She understands what we're trying to find out, so she'll call me as soon as she has a more solid theory. Meantime, *mes amis*,[11] what do you suggest the four of us do until we hear from her?"

"There's really not much we can do until we hear from

---

11. my friends

your captain, *Guy* and the twins about their session with the count." Cincinnati said. "Maybe we should check with Socks at the C.I.A. in the White House basement to see if she's picked up any more telephone calls from her satellite."

Dusty looked confused. "Cincinnati, it's 9:00 in the morning here. So it's about 3:00 A.M. in Washington. Are you sure you want to call Socks now? It's just a question, not really an emergency, right?"

"I sure don't want to call her," Buzzer said. "Not before about 2:00 this afternoon."

René had a thought and clapped his front paws together. "I know what we can do," he said. "Let's all go and have a nice, quiet French breakfast. The *Brigade Criminelle* will be our host."

✳ ✳ ✳

Back at the Café Madeleine

The count was telling a long and somewhat confusing story. "So my great-great-grandfather, Franz Joseph, to get even for the terrible French army attack on a little village in what is now northern Italy, but was then western Austria, had Paris surrounded. The roads were closed off. No boat traffic passed into the city on the Seine. Once all the food was gone and the people of Paris were having to eat rats, Franz Joseph was satisfied that he'd made his point. So he ordered his troops to withdraw."

"Sounds like a decent thing to do," Luigi said. "Why starve all of Paris?"

"Exactly, Nick. He was a great warrior, but he was also a gallant man. The punishment for the attack of the French army was sufficient without mass starvation, no?" the count answered.

"What went wrong?" Luisa asked.

"Well, Nikki," the count answered, "what went wrong was that a pig-headed French official decided to further his political career, and so announced in a loud and obnoxious voice that the valor of the people of Paris had driven the Austro-Hungarian forces from France and back to Vienna."

Guy looked and sounded sympathetic. "That was a terrible lie, no? As a descendant of the great Franz Joseph, I'm not happy to hear this story. Not happy at all. In fact," he went on, nodding at Luigi, "it almost makes me want to fight—to avenge the honor of my family."

Luigi jumped in immediately. "This terrible wrong has to be righted. It just can't be left to history. For the sake of our old great-great-grandfather."

Luisa added, "Yes. *Absolument, sans doute!*[12] We have to do something about it right away. But what can we do?" Turning to Count von Stuffel, she asked, "Count, surely you must have some thoughts on how we can get even. After all, you've known about this terrible thing for many years, and you've had a lot of time to think about it. We just heard it for the first time today. What can we do?"

The count looked around nervously. He checked the others in the restaurant, excused himself to look into the kitchen and the bathrooms. When he returned to the table, he leaned toward Nick and Nikki and asked, "Can you keep a secret? A very big and important secret?" *Guy* looked at

---

12. "Absolutely. Without doubt!"

Luigi. Luigi looked at Luisa. Then all three looked at Count von Stuffel, thinking, *Here comes the payoff. This nincompoop is about to solve our mystery for us. His ego's bigger than his common sense.*

The count whispered, "I've hired a big cat from South America to avenge the honor of Franz Joseph. It's costing me 5,000,000 Euros, but soon we will have our revenge. And the world will know the truth at last."

Guy, Luigi and Luisa all stared at the count without blinking.

"*Continue,*[13] cousin," *Guy* said. "What is this big cat going to do?"

"And when?" Luigi asked, as Luisa said, "Where?"

Again the count looked carefully around the restaurant and out onto *le trottoir et la rue.*[14] He leaned even farther across the table to speak just above a whisper. "The cat won't tell me the details. Only that he's hired twelve Gypsies to help him. I believe their job will be to create a lot of mostly harmless confusion. You know, cause the authorities to scramble here and there on what you Americans might call 'wild goose chases,' no?"

Luigi pressed him. "So what is this big cat going to do while the Gypsies are causing confusion all over town?" He had another question, although he already knew the answer. "Will this big cat be the one who gets the real revenge?"

The count said, "Yes. It will be the cat, himself."

---

13. Go on
14. the sidewalk and the street

Luisa asked quickly, "What's he going to do? How can one cat get even by himself?"

Luigi added, "And when is he going to do whatever it is he's planning?"

"He will destroy the monument the Parisians built in gratitude for the *faux*[15] victory they claim over Franz Joseph."

"And where will you be when this happens, cousin?" *Guy* asked.

"I won't be in Paris. I'm leaving tomorrow afternoon for my summer home near Munich. In Bavaria."

"So the big cat will be avenging us the next day?" Luigi asked.

"Yes. On *Bastille* Day, when there is already a lot of confusion on the streets of Paris," the count said.

The pieces of the puzzle were coming together, but Luisa had just one more question. "Do you know exactly what he's going to destroy on that day?"

"Yes, of course," the count said. "It's what I'm paying him to do. The Gypsies and whatever they're going to do were his idea. I know nothing about that. When I talked to him yesterday, he said I didn't need to know any more."

"What else did he say?" *Guy* asked.

Suddenly the count looked sick. In fact, he looked as though he might pass out and fall off his chair any second.

"He warned me to keep quiet," he said. "He actually threatened me. I can't say another word. I've already said enough to get me into real trouble."

---

15. faux is a French word often used in English. It means fake or phony.

"*Ne t'enquiétes pas, cousin,*"[15] Guy said quietly and reassuringly. "After all, we're family, and we want this big cat to be successful every bit as much as you do. So why don't you tell us what he's going to destroy. I'll even pay half his fee. How much is that, Nick or Nikki?"

Luisa answered quickly, "About three or four million U.S. dollars, Dad."

Guy faked shock and added quickly, "Maybe I can only pay three million dollars, cousin. But I can do that. If you will share the location with us. Remember, we are as angry about this injustice as you are."

Count von Stuffel looked at each of his new-found relatives. *They seem to be honest and caring. I think I believe them. But I should think about it some more.*

"I have to go now," he said, hurriedly excusing himself. "But I'll think about your question. Why don't you meet me here for breakfast at 8:00 in the morning? If I can, I'll tell you the location. If not, I'll tell you why I can't. After all, we are family, no?"

With that he jumped from his chair and hurried out the front door.

Guy clapped his front paws together and said softly, "The fool spilled almost all the beans."

Instantly, both waved a paw at him, and Luisa whispered sternly, "Not here, *Guy*. Not now!"

Luigi added quickly, "I think I prefer the *quiche* recipe to the *crepes*. But they were all good. Let's put three different recipes into the cartons of eggs. It will be good to rotate them."

---

15. "Don't worry, cousin."

"Great idea, Nikki," Luisa said in a normal voice. "Let's go back to the hotel now. I'll bet there'll be some others who'll want to know how our little breakfast experiment went."

Do you think the count will tell our heroes at breakfast in the morning where Carlos is going to do his destruction? What do you think will happen to the count if Carlos finds out he's been telling the Brigade Criminelle and the C.I.A. about his plans? Do you think the twelve Gypsies will be dependable and create as much confusion as Carlos wants? And what about Luigi and Luisa—do you think they're really vegetarians?

Parlez Vous Francais?
by Cincinnati

If you're ever in Paris, you might want to take some short trips outside the city to places like *Versailles* or *Normandy*. *Comment dite vous quel moyen de transport avez-vous besoin?*[16]

English	French	Say It Like This
Subway	*Métro*	meh-TROH
Taxi	*Taxi*	tax-EE
Airplane	*Avion*	ah-VYOHN
Train	*Train*	TREH(n)
Car	*Voiture*	vwah-TEUR
Police car	*Voiture de Police*	vwah-TEUR deh poh-LEESZ
Ship	*Bateau*	bah-TOH
Bus	*Autobus*	autoh-BEUSZ
Boat	*Barque*	BARK
Truck	*Camion*	cah-MYOH(n)
Pickup	*Pickup*	PICKUP
Bicycle	*Bicyclette*	bee-see-CLEHT
Helicopter	*Hélicoptère*	ehl-ee-chop-TAIR
Road/highway	*Route/Autoroute*	ROOT/au-toh-ROOT
Street	*Rue*	REU
River	*Fleuve*	FLUV
Sea	*Mer*	MAIR
Stream	*Ruisseau*	ree-SZEAU
Sidewalk	*Trottoir*	troh-TWAH(r)
Path	*Chemin*	sheh-MEH(n)
Airport	*Aéroport*	air-oh-POHR

---

16. How will you say what kind of transportation you'll need?

* Chapter 17 *
Le plan secret découvert[1]

René's Office at the Brigade Criminelle

"What do you think the chances are that this nutty count lied to you just to throw us off the track?" Cincinnati asked *Guy* and the twins.

"That would assume he knew who we really were," *Guy* answered.

Luisa added, "No, Cincinnati, he was so anxious to be a big-shot in front of his long-lost cousin that his ego got the better of his common sense. He thought we were somebody we weren't, just as we planned, and he spilled everything he knew. Except, of course, the exact location where Carlos will do whatever it is he's planning to do."

"What do you think, Luigi?" Cincinnati asked.

"He's a doofus. This character has more phobias and manias than a psychiatrist's desk reference guide. The only thing I'm at all concerned about is what he might just have

---

1. Secret Plan Uncovered

made up. Did he tell us more than he really knows? Maybe."

"Okay, then," Buzzer said, "his story matches the guesstimate _René's_ captain-historian has pulled together. I don't believe in coincidences. Carlos's hired a dozen Gypsies to create a huge diversion all over the city on a major holiday when all of Paris will already be on the streets. While those diversions, whatever they are, keep the authorities very busy and maybe even set off widespread panic, Carlos himself blows up some building or monument that will supposedly get even with the people of Paris for some ridiculous slight that must have happened more than a hundred years ago."

René said softly, "_Sacre bleu! Quel planificateur intelligent_[2] this Carlos must be."

"Oh, yes, he's clever all right," Buzzer said. "But thanks to the disguise Luigi and Luisa devised for _Guy_, I think we're once again a step ahead of him."

Dusty spoke up for the first time. "Let's recap what we know, or think we know. Luigi?" She turned the discussion over to her little brother, much to his and Luisa's amazement.

"Here's where we are," Luigi began. "We know this much: The action will take place on _Bastille_ Day, _le jour après demain_.[3] There will be diversions, at least 12 of them, to add to the confusion already on the streets—the people, the fireworks, the hot air balloons, the kites. And the diversions will be spectacular, but mostly harmless—_le faux attaque_.[4]

---

2. "Blue blood! What a clever planner"
3. the day after tomorrow.
4. a fake attack

We can practically ignore them. Except the thirteenth will be for real. And that's where Carlos will be."

He turned to Luisa," What else?" he asked.

"Well, Luisa said, "this Count Cockamamie knows two things that are important: first, where Carlos is hiding out and planning—remember he said he talked to 'the big cat' yesterday; and, second, what and where, exactly, the real target is. Because he chose that target, and it has something to do with somebody slighting Franz Joseph four generations ago."

René asked *Guy*, "Do you think the count will tell you at breakfast tomorrow what the real target is supposed to be?"

Guy answered, "*Peut être que oui, peut être que non. Je ne sais pas.*"[5]

Luigi jumped in, "Cousin *René*, one of two things will happen in the morning. Either the count just won't show up, or he'll be so full of bluster he'll give us the place, the zip code, the exact address and the GPS coordinates."

Luisa added, "Yes. With him it's going to be *tout ou rien.*"[6]

Buzzer summed up their position. "If we can't count on *all*, then we'd better plan on *nothing.*"

Cincinnati turned to *René*. "Can you check with your captain at the library at the *Sorbonne* to see if she's been able to connect the end of Franz's siege with the building of some kind of monument? If we can get those two dots connected, we might just have found Carlos' target. Then, in the morning, the count will either show up and confirm

---

5. "Maybe. Maybe not. I don't know."
6. all or nothing

we're right, or he'll skip town and head back for Munich earlier than he'd planned.

"Here are the facts. We'll either have a confirmed target or our best estimate of the target. Make sense?"

René said. "I'll call her again." He stepped into his office and rushed for the phone.

"Is anybody hungry?" Luigi asked. "Besides me?"

"Didn't you just have an elegant breakfast two hours ago?" Dusty said.

"We were there at an elegant breakfast, Dusty, but we were both working," Luisa answered. "We were concentrating. Neither of us really ate a bite."

"And it did look so good," Luigi added.

René walked quickly back into the conference room, looking excited.

"*Marlene* says she thinks she may have the answer. She's on her way here now," he said.

❋ ❋ ❋

In Carlos's Suite at the Paris Ritz

Carlos sipped on a cup of hot French-roast coffee and snacked on a plate of miniature *éclairs*[7] as he read for the fourth or fifth time a small booklet titled *Assembling and Flying the Acme Delta*. Before the afternoon was over, he would memorize the eleven steps from "Removing the Delta from its carrying case" to "Launching flight from heights."

---

7. *Éclair* is another French word we use in everyday English. It's a custard filled pastry.

The "kit" Carlos had asked his pilots about and told them where to stash was the *Acme Delta*, a compact, collapsible ultra-light aircraft made for one person—the pilot. Carlos had ordered it from Brazil when he was in prison, thinking he might ask his assistants to smuggle it near the prison walls and then be able to escape by flying out. However, the jungle around the prison had been too thick. There was not enough open space to take off.

This time, though, he had a perfect place to launch the motor-powered kite—the top of a tall building on the top of a big hill. He would simply snap it together on the roof, fire up the little 300 cc engine and, strapped into the pilot's harness, jump off the building and fly away into skies already crowded with hot air balloons, regular kites, hang gliders, and a few other ultra-lights like his own *Acme Delta*.

The perfect escape.

And he would be miles away before the massive explosion completely demolished the roof he'd used for a launch platform.

A perfect getaway.

Carlos was no amateur when it came to flying ultra-lights. He had learned and trained carefully by flying his *Acme Delta* on the Atlantic beaches south of Buenos Aires. Once he had amassed about ten hours' time piloting the little kite-like plane, he practiced launches from rooftops and mountain tops. So that he would be prepared for anything, he had flown the little craft in the Antarctic and in mild tropical thundershowers—against the advice of the craft's manufacturer and both of his own pilots.

Now Carlos was ready. Whatever the weather on *Bastille*

Day, however crowded the skies, he had the little aircraft and the piloting experience to get away cleanly from Paris.

Adieu, Ville de lumières. Tu auras un faux monument de moin. Bientôt.[8]

✻ ✻ ✻

Headquarters of Brigade Criminelle—René's Conference Room

René ordered in a big platter of *sandwiches*[9] and bottles of Perrier® water so the group could continue working through lunch. They were eating and listening, which was not always easy for Luigi and Luisa. Especially when they were really hungry.

Captaine Marlene,[10] *René's* fourth company commander, had arrived and was explaining her findings on the history of Franz Joseph's siege and retreat from Paris.

"So you see, *mes amis d'Amerique,*[11] when Franz Joseph left with his troops for Vienna and Budapest, the people of Paris were grateful the siege was over. Of course, they had been told the French army had driven the Austro-Hungarians from Paris by force, and so had won a great victory. That was not exactly true, but it served the needs of local politicians.

"In gratitude for the great victory and the food that now flowed without problems into the city, the people of Paris began collecting funds to build a great basilica—a monument to a false victory over the Austro-Hungarians."

---

8. "Goodbye, City of Lights. You'll have one less false monument. Soon."
9. sandwiches
10. Captain Marlene
11. my friends from America

"*Notre Dame?*" Dusty blurted out.

"Not *Notre Dame,*" Luigi said, and immediately wanted to take his words back. *Why didn't I let someone else correct Dusty?* he thought.

Captain *Marlene* smiled at Dusty and said, ever so gently, "*Non, Madame, pas Notre Dame.*"[12] *Notre Dame* is many hundreds of years older. This monument is on top of the highest hill in Paris."

"*Sacre Coeur,*"[13] Luisa said, her eyes growing as wide as walnuts. "We were just there two nights ago. You can see the whole city from up there."

"*Oui, petite,*[14] *Sacre Coeur Basilica*. That's the monument to the relief of the siege of Paris by Franz Joseph," the captain said.

"Ground zero!" Luigi shouted.

"*Excuse moi?*"[15] *Guy* said. "What you mean by this 'ground zero?'"

Luisa smiled. "In the business of doing in criminals, *Guy*, you'll want to call the place where you plan to capture bad guys 'ground zero.' If you're going to be a secret agent, you need to remember that."

"This all makes perfect sense, in a goofy kind of way," Cincinnati said. "So this nut, the count, wants to make the people of Paris today pay for the lies of Parisian politicians four generations ago? Weird, truly weird."

"I can easily believe it, even though it makes little sense to anybody who can think," Luigi said. "Most of you

12. "No, Madam, not Notre Dame."
13. *Sacre Coeur Basilica*. Literally, Sacred Heart Basilica.
14. Yes, little one
15. "Excuse me?"

haven't spent a couple of hours with this Count von Stuffel like Luisa, Guy and I have. Does it seem believable to you, Luisa?"

"Absolutely. The count's a bundle of neuroses, psychoses, and paranoias. He has some strangely-driven notion that's he's been chosen to avenge his ancestors."

"A Savior complex," Cincinnati offered.

"Exactly," Buzzer said, adding, "So, if the famous *Sacre Coeur* is 'ground zero,' as Luigi and Luisa and all secret agents everywhere would call it, what are the most likely decoy targets—the ones where the Gypsies will cause a momentary commotion?"

"Good question, Buzzer," *René* answered. "Let's take a short break while I retrieve a map of the city. We'll need to pinpoint as many as the twenty or so most prominent monuments, just to be safe.

"Meanwhile, how about a small round of applause for Captain *Marlene? Vous avez fait un travail magnifique, Captaine.*[16] But don't breathe a word to anyone outside this room. Not yet. Secret instructions will come down through the chain of command in the morning. You and the other captains will each be told what your companies will need to do on *Bastille* Day."

✻ ✻ ✻

The Apartment of the Count Freidrich von Stuffel

The count paced back and forth across the parlor of his posh apartment on the *Champs Elysee*. Eleven-and-a-half

---

16. "Magnificent work, Captain."

paces northeast to the window overlooking the boulevard below, turn, eleven-and-a-half paces southwest to the French doors leading to his formal dining room. Back and forth. Back and forth.

He'd turned on no lights, but the sun had begun peeping into the southwest window in the early afternoon. The count had been walking for hours. Ever since his brain had returned to rational toward the end of his breakfast with his long-lost cousins from America and Oxford.

What have I done? I've talked too much, that's what. Yes, I shouldn't have told Gary and the twins about Carlos. Did I mention his name? I don't think so. But what does it matter? How many big pumas from Argentina, who are also terrorists, can there be?

Back and forth he paced. *Then, again, Gary's just a farmer who squeezes eggs out of hens. Lots of hens, millions of eggs. What does he know of our great-great-grandfather? I think nothing. Or not much.*

Back and forth, back and forth he paced. Arguing with himself.

Carlos warned me not to talk. He told me never to cross Carlos the puma, or there would be consequences. Did I really cross him? I don't think so. But he might think so. And if he does, I might end up at the bottom of the Seine, wrapped in chains. Food for the fish.

What can I do about it now? Should I do anything? Or would that just make things worse? Maybe the best thing is to do nothing. Meet with Gary and his twins again in the morning and pretend the whole thing was just a joke. Would that work? Maybe my long-lost cousin is too bent on revenge now that I've told him the real story.

Maybe I'll just meet with them, and take their 3,000,000 dollars, say 'Thank you,' and then disappear.

Disappear? That's the answer! I need to disappear. Right after I wire the other 2,500,000 Euros to Carlos's banks. That's what I'll do! Pay up and disappear. If the puma has his money—all of it—he won't come after me. Will he? Stupid, stupid, stupid! Why do I care about Franz Joseph and his reputation, anyway? Did he ever do anything for me? The Austro-Hungarian Empire has been kaput for almost a hundred years, anyway. But now I have a plan: Pay up. Disappear.

At that, he stopped pacing and sat down. But the perspiration kept running down his face and neck.

After a moment, he reached for the phone. First he would call his pilots and tell them to get his plane ready to leave for Munich. *By what time? It's 2:00 now. The sooner the better. Make it 4:30 at Orly Airport.* Then he'd call his bankers in Zurich, have them send Carlos the rest of his money.

I know, he thought. *I'll send an extra million Euros as a "thank you" for a job well done in blowing up Sacre Coeur. Or would it be to keep him from coming after me? Would the extra money make him mad? He said he lives by his word and his price. If I send him extra money, he might try to return it. In person.*

Okay, okay. No extra money. Too much could go wrong. Just the 2,500,000 Euros we agreed on. Then I'm out of here.

What will happen when the count fails to show up for the scheduled breakfast in the morning? What do you think Carlos will do to him if he finds out the count's been talking too much? What if Carlos finds out that Gary Gonzachu and Nick and Nikki are really Guy Gondeaux *of the* Brigade Criminelle *and Luigi and Luisa of the secret* Cats In Action? *And how will our heroes get ready for the attacks that are coming on* Bastille Day? *Will the Gypsies get in trouble if they don't really do any damage? And what is the business between the count and* Remy Dewclaux *all about, anyway? Is* Remy, *the head of all French spies, a double agent?*

Parlez Vous Francais?

by Cincinnati

There are lots of very smart animals doing secret work around the world. If you wanted to be a secret agent in France, *quels noms donnerait-vous aux autres animaux agents?* [17]

English	French	Say It Like This
Cat	Chat	SHAH
Kitten	Petit chat	peht-EE-shah
Dog	Chien	SHIEN
Bird	Ouiseau	wah-SZOH
Donkey	Ane	AHN
Pig	Cochon	coh-SHOH(n)
Parrot	Perroquet	pair-oh-KAY
Bear	Ours	OARSZ
Eagle	Aigle	AY-gleh
Tiger	Tigre	TEE-Greh
Turtle	Tortoise	tohr-TWASZ
Wolf	Loup	LOO
Snake	Serpent	sair-PAH(n)
Fox	Renard	reh-NAHR
Horse	Cheval	sheh-VAHL
Cow	Vache	vah-SH
Sheep	Mouton	moo-TOH(n)
Goat	Chèvre	SHEH-vreh
Skunk	Moufette	moo-FETT
Lion	Lion	lee-OH(n)
Fish	Poisson	pwah-SOH(n)
Cougar	Puma	POO-mah

---

17. What names would you call the other animal agents?

* Chapter 18 *
Attrapez cet chat[1]

René's Office—Brigade Criminelle Headquarters

"Okay, Buzzer, you and Cincinnati have more experience than anybody else with this Carlos character, so why don't you outline what you think we should do tomorrow to get ready for him on *Bastille* Day?" *René* suggested.

Buzzer looked to Cincinnati, who nodded 'yes.'

"I think, *René*," Buzzer began, "the smart work of Luigi and Luisa and *Guy* have gotten us this far—to a pretty good understanding of what Carlos is up to and how he's going to go about it. Why don't we let them give us their ideas? Cincinnati and Dusty and I can fill in the blanks, if there are any."

Buzzer turned to the twins, who were looking at one another with huge smiles on their faces. "What about it, you two? Do we need Ma and Pa Kettle day after tomorrow?"

Luisa began with a question for *René*. "Can you get some manpower help from the *Prefecture de Police*?"[2]

---

1. Catch That Cat
2. Police Department

"Certainly, if we're careful whom we work through. There are some I simply don't trust, but we don't have to deal with those. So, yes, Luisa, we can."

The twins then began to tick off their strategy, point by point, taking turns listing each tactic, being careful to look to *Guy* at the end of each statement:

🐾 "First, we need two officers on site at each of the twenty most likely locations for the diversions, starting at 8:00 A.M. These officers are to watch for Gypsies doing odd or suspicious things. We suggest one policeman and one of your *Brigade Criminelle* agents—in pairs. That's twenty cops and twenty agents," Luigi said.

🐾 "They're to observe the Gypsies, but not stop them unless they're absolutely sure somebody might get hurt. Remember, these targets, whichever ones they may be, are supposed to be harmless diversions. Let the Gypsies do what they're hired to do so Carlos will think his plan is working; then pick them up if you wish," Luisa said.

🐾 "The police and the *pompier*[3] commands need to be told about what's happening—not to just jump and run willy-nilly every time somebody reports a noise or some smoke—at a major monument," Luigi added. "We don't want to add to whatever confusion Carlos can start by having emergency vehicles running around everywhere."

---

3. fire department

🐾 "Also, we need the four best agents you have, plus a paddy wagon, pepper spray, a burlap bag and a straitjacket to join us in *Montmartre* at the base of the big stairway to *Sacre Coeur* at about 7:00 A.M. We'll be watching the cathedral from all sides. Be sure the paddy wagon is disguised as a delivery truck, and the agents are dressed as if on holiday," Luisa said.

🐾 "Finally," Luigi added, "we'll need binoculars for each of us and each agent, portable two-way radios, a stand-by helicopter disguised as an air ambulance for Cincinnati and Dusty to fly in case we need someone up above as spotters for the team on the ground. And two Vespas, please." Luigi grinned at Luisa.

Dusty spoke up. "Forget the Vespas, *René*. These two always ask for two *scooters*[4] so they can ride them all over the place when the action's over." Turning to the twins, she said, "Nice try, but no cigar. Or Vespas."

Luigi couldn't resist. "How about a couple of skateboards, then?"

Luisa laughed, but Dusty did not.

"Anything else?" *René* turned to Buzzer and Cincinnati.

"Not yet," Buzzer answered. "You and *Guy* have enough to do already. Just tell us how we can help while you're making your contacts and setting up your teams—and briefing them."

---

4. motor scooters

Guy spoke up. Hearing him speak out no longer seemed strange to the others.

"Can those of you with the Cats In Action go to *Sacre Coeur* and plot out exactly where each of us and the other agents need to be? Also what we need to be watching, and watching for?"

"Consider it done," Cincinnati said. "And we'll see you here first thing in the morning to compare notes and to be sure all the bases are covered."

"*Très bien*," René said. "*A toute l'heure.*"[5]

* * *

July 12—A Busy Afternoon

Les Chats and Cincinnati the dancing pig took the Metro to *Sacre Coeur*, where they walked around all sides of the cathedral, climbed to the top of its big dome and figured out exactly how and where to shut off any possible escape Carlos might try. Luigi and Luisa even made an aerial-view drawing of the entire area and marked where the agent teams each should be.

Cincinnati and Dusty would remain at street level below the hill with a taxi, standing by in case they needed to get to the helicopter that *René* would have positioned on the roof of a building several blocks away.

Buzzer and the twins would be in the top of the dome, patrolling around a catwalk inside so they could see what was happening in all directions below.

Satisfied that all escape routes would be covered, they

---

5. "Very good. See you then."

went back to their suite at the *Georges Cinq* to get some rest. They knew the next two days would be long and tiring.

✻ ✻ ✻

Back with the Count

Meanwhile, Count Freidrich von Stuffel headed for Orly airport, his plane and a quick trip back to his base of operations in Munich. On the way to the plane, he called Carlos from his car phone. When the big puma answered, the count spoke. "I'm just calling to wish you and your Gypsies *bonne chance le jour après demain.*[6] Unfortunately, my business interests require me to leave Paris today."

"*Pas de problème,*[7] Count," Carlos said. "You're not needed here. In fact, you never have been needed here. I asked you when I called you from Marrakech not to come to Paris at all. There's now a record you've been here for the last two days. That will not be helpful. So it's best for you to be far away as soon as possible. Where are you going?"

Count von Stuffel thought quickly. "I have to be in Hong Kong tomorrow afternoon," he said. "Halfway around the world."

"Excellent. Now, what about the second half of my payment?" Carlos asked.

"It has been taken care of. Receipts will be faxed to your offices in Argentina by noon on *Bastille* Day."

"I may not be quite finished by noon, Count," Carlos answered.

---

6. good luck the day after tomorrow
7. No problem

The count decided to try a little flattery. "As you've said, my big cat friend, 'Carlos never fails.' I'll talk to you next week."

"No, Count, you won't. You'll never talk to Carlos again. You've never seen me. In fact, you have no idea who I am. Never heard of me. Unless, of course, you've somehow compromised this job. Or unless you fail to pay the second half of our agreed-upon sum, in which case you'll truly wish you'd never heard of Carlos. Are we clear on that, Count?"

The line went dead.

Still holding the phone, the big puma thought, *The count is a weakling with crazy century-old vendettas. He's too stupid to know nobody will care about his revenge after it's all over, anyway. And he's too timid to do his own dirty work. What a fool. But a rich fool, and one who'll make Carlos even richer.*

Carlos called the concierge. "Please send up a large salad, a bowl of mushroom soup, an extra large vegetable platter, two *bouteilles d'eaux—gaseuse*,[8] and two scoops of ice cream. And ask the front desk to hold my calls for twenty hours—until noon tomorrow. The diamond salesman is going to sleep."

Until he's totally rested. And it's time for the fun to begin.

Why do you think Carlos wants to sleep for twenty hours after eating a hearty meal? Do you think the count freaked out when Carlos threatened him on the phone? Is that why he hung up the phone? And why did he tell Carlos that he's on the way to Hong Kong and those other lies—that the money hadn't been sent to Carlos' accounts, but would be sent on Bastille *Day? Will* René

---

8. bottles of water—with gas (carbonated)

and Guy get the help they need from the Paris Police Department? Do you think the Gypsies should be arrested even if they don't do any damage or hurt anyone? What, exactly, are they planning to do, anyway? And what of Luigi and Luisa's tactical plan? Is it thorough enough?

Parlez Vous Français
by Cincinnati

Since it looks like Carlos is going to blow up a basilica, *quels sont les mots français que vous voudriez utiliser parlant d'une église?*[9]

English	French	Say It Like This
Church	*Église*	eg-LEESZ
Cathedral	*Cathèdral*	caht-eh-DRAHL
Pews	*Bancs d'eglise*	bah(n) deh GLEESZ
Candles	*Chandelles*	shohn-DELLE
Pulpit	*Chaire*	SHARE
Nave	*Nef*	NEF
Confessional	*Confessional*	cohn-fess-eh-oh-NAHL
Sacraments	*Sacrements*	sah-creh-MOH(n)
Choir	*Choeur*	CUER
Priest	*Prêtre*	PRET-reh
Basilica	*Basilique*	bahs-il-EEK
Organ	*Orgue*	OHRGH
Prayer	*Prière*	PREE-air

---

9. What are the French words you'd use to talk about a church?

* Chapter 19 *
Le jour de la Bastille[1]

In the Dome of Sacre Coeur Basilica—7:00 A.M.

René and *Guy* had placed four *Brigade Criminelle* agents on the ground exactly where Buzzer and Cincinnati had said they should be—according to the map Luigi and Luisa had drawn.

Buzzer, Luigi and Luisa, along with *René*, walked slowly around the catwalk near the top of the big church's dome, watching the ground below for any sign of Carlos.

Guy had been sent to meet with the bishop at *Notre Dame* Cathedral and with the priests of *Sacre Coeur* to tell them of the danger and to let them know there would be few visitors to *Sacre Coeur* that morning. The aerial tramway from the street up to the cathedral had an *"Hors service"*[2] sign on it, and barricades blocked the big pedestrian stairways. Each stairway's barricade also had a sign that read *"Temporairement fermé. Construction dangereuse."*[3]

---

1. Bastille Day
2. Out of Order

3. Closed temporarily. Dangerous construction

Cincinnati and Dusty waited down on the street in the back seat of a taxi—the one that would take them quickly to the air-ambulance helicopter if they were needed as spotters in the sky.

"Have you seen anything yet?" Luisa asked her twin brother as they passed one another on their paths around *Sacre Coeur*'s big dome.

"Not yet," Luigi answered. "But it's still pretty early."

Looking out one of the dome's windows, Buzzer saw what looked to him like an oversized duffel bag lying on the flat roof of the basilica below the dome. He waited for René to make his way around the round dome to where he was standing.

"What do you think that is, *René*" he asked his cousin in the red beret. "It wasn't here *le jour avant hier*[4] when the twins, Dusty and Cincinnati and I were here plotting our positions for this morning."

René looked down. "Looks like a big blue bag to me," *René* said. "I'll have *Guy* check it out when he gets back from talking to the *évêque et les prêtres*."[5] He pulled out his cell phone to call his newly intelligent assistant to ask him to check the big bag on the roof and also to remind him to bring the two bomb squad experts from the *Prefecture de Police*[6] on up into the dome when they arrived in a few minutes.

* * *

---

4. the day before yesterday
5. bishop and the priests
6. Police Department

At the Paris Ritz Hotel

Carlos was checking out at the front desk and retrieving his sample case from the hotel's safe. He'd taken it out again yesterday afternoon to get a dozen smoke bombs he'd rigged up for the Gypsies as a part of the diversion that would start in less than an hour. Instead of diamond samples, though, it now contained only C-4 plastic explosives, fuses and detonator caps, his tools for destroying the monument to the *faux* French victory over Franz Joseph in the 1870s.

"When will you favor us with another visit, Mr. Diamond Salesman?" his old friend the desk clerk asked, adding, "I trust you've found this stay a good experience."

"Yes, the Paris Ritz today is as comfortable and fine as ever. My business in Paris is finished for now," Carlos said. "So I'm headed for Moscow in a couple of hours. Can't keep those Ruskies with all their new-found wealth waiting, no? They demand diamonds, and more diamonds of the finest quality. The kind that only I can deliver."

He scratched his chin. "I'm not sure when I'll be back here but *tu peus en être sur*[7] I'll be staying with you once again. *Au revoir, pour le moment.*"[8]

With that he went through the revolving front door to his big black Mercedes and his driver waiting to drop him off in Montmartre, in front of a McDonald's down the street and around the corner from his target, *Sacre Coeur*.

From there he would stroll casually to a nearby building

---

7. You may be sure.
8. Goodbye, for now.

where he'd go to the roof to keep an eye out for the results of the Gypsies' work. And watch *Sacre Coeur* until it was time for him to go there—at noon.

What he didn't expect was to find an apparently abandoned helicopter air ambulance on that roof. He would puzzle over that find for just a moment, but quickly return to the concentration on his mission that had made him the best terrorist in the world.

* * *

Back in the Dome of the Basilica—8:45 A.M.

Guy and the two members of the Paris Police bomb squad climbed into the dome. *Guy* looked around for Buzzer and *René*.

"The bishop and the priests are warned," he said. "And these two gentlemen are adept at defusing bombs. As for blue bag you spotted on the roof below goes, it was locked. We used instruments to be sure it contained no explosives, and it didn't. But we could detect the faint smell of gasoline and motor oil. It's perhaps some kind of machine, but without breaking into it, we can't tell exactly what."

"Let's just keep an eye on it, then," Buzzer said. "It may be completely harmless."

Luigi finished a radio check with each of the twenty pairs of police and *Brigade Criminelle* lookouts posted at the twenty most likely targets around the city. "Radio's all working and ready," he announced. "But nothing's happened yet."

* * *

9:00 A.M.—The Basilica Dome

Luisa was first to see the dense black smoke rising in the south on the left bank of the Seine. "Big smoke!" she shouted, "Almost straight south."

Just then the radio Luigi was monitoring crackled, "*Hotel des Invalides*[9] to *Sacre Coeur*," a voice came over the radio. "We have a smoke bomb here. Just a lot of thick black smoke that smells bad."

Luigi keyed the microphone and asked, "Any explosion? Any casualties? Any damage?"

"No," came the reply. "Just a loud hiss and a lot of smoke. We have a Gypsy woman in custody. We actually saw her trip the smoke bomb."

René spoke into his radio. "*Bien fait.*"[10] This is Commander *Fopaux*. Take the Gypsy into custody and take a detailed statement from her. Charge her with disorderly conduct and, if she cooperates, let her go until her court date."

Luisa asked quickly, "You want to let her go? Why not keep her in jail—at least until we have Carlos rounded up."

Seeing *René* was very busy, *Guy* answered. "Disorderly conduct is a simple crime—a misdemeanor. As long as she did no damage and nobody was hurt, she'll get off with a small fine, anyway. Besides, she won't be back on the streets for several hours. Perhaps until as late as sundown. She isn't a danger any longer."

"If she ever really was," Luisa added, understanding why it didn't make any sense to try to keep her in jail.

---

9. Hotel of the Invalids. A former hotel for disabled soldiers that houses Napoleon's tomb.
10. "Good work."

* * *

9:15 A.M.—Basilica Dome

Luigi was first to spot the next eruption. "Smoke again to the south," he said, "this time a little east of the first smoke bomb."

"Probably the *Champ du Mars Park*," René suggested.

Sure enough, the radio crackled again. "*Champ du Mars* to *Sacre Coeur*, we have another smoke bomb. Out in the open. No damage. No injuries. Just an awful stink."

Luigi keyed his microphone, "Did you see any Gypsies set off the smoke?"

"No," came the reply. "There are thousands of people here. They're *se tiennent leurs nez fermés*[11] and going about their celebrations almost as if almost nothing's happened. Typical Parisian attitude."

"*Merci*,"[12] René spoke into the radio. "You may both go back to your normal duties. Just keep your eyes and ears open."

Luigi added quickly into his radio, "It's okay to close your noses, though."

Luisa laughed.

Buzzer and *René* were off to the side talking quietly. "Let's give it one more time—one more smoke bomb. Then we'll pull the plug on any fear or panic these little bombs might be causing," Buzzer said.

"Agreed," *René* answered.

---

11. holding their noses.
12. "Thank you"

* * *

9:30 A.M.—Basilica Dome

"New smoke bomb," Guy shouted. "Looks like the top of the *Eiffel Tower* this time. Way up in the air."

René turned to Luigi. "Contact the *Eiffel Tower* team if you don't hear from them in the next thirty seconds. You know what to tell them."

Buzzer turned to *Guy.* "Get hold of the Public Information Office at the *Prefecture de Police.* Have them contact all the broadcast media at once. Tell them this: 'The police and fire departments are conducting some routine tests of response times during heavy holiday traffic. There will be periodic, harmless smoke bombs set off at fifteen-minute intervals for most of the morning. The public doesn't need to pay any attention to them.

"Then contact the fire chief and the police chief. Ask them to have a couple of emergency vehicles run up and down the streets, circling all over town with lights flashing and sirens wailing—just to make the story of routine response time drills more believable. Can you do that, *Guy*? *S'il te plait?*"[13]

Sure enough, every fifteen minutes another harmless but smelly smoke bomb went off, each one creeping closer to *Sacre Coeur.*

🐾 9:45 A.M.—   In the *Trocadero,* across the *Seine* from the *Eiffel Tower.*

---

13. Please?

🐾 10:00 A.M.— At *Notre Dame*, on an island in the *Seine*

🐾 10:15 A.M.— At the *Musee du Louvre*

🐾 10:30 A.M.— At the Musee D'Orsay, on the left bank across from the Louvre

🐾 10:45 A.M.— At the Grand Palais, former residence of the head of state

Every quarter hour, the smoke bombs went off. The smoke eruptions crept closer and closer to *Sacre Coeur*; *Arc d' Triomphe* on the *Champs Elysee*; *Opera Galleries Lafayette*.

At 11:45, with ten smoke bombs already detonated, Buzzer called everyone in the Dome together.

"He's almost here," he said. "There should be two more smoke bombs, even closer this time. And then, fifteen minutes later, Carlos will try to blow this building up. So here's what we're going to do."

* * *

The Roof of a Nearby Building

Carlos was pleased. He'd seen ten smoke bombs explode exactly on schedule. The Gypsies had done their jobs perfectly. Now it was time for him to finish his work. No need to wait for the twelfth smoke bomb. It didn't really matter now if it went off or not.

Carlos the puma took in a deep breath, picked up his sample case and left the roof of the building and the strange, abandoned helicopter air ambulance. Downstairs, he walked to the corner and turned into the edge of a park, approaching an entrance to the sewers that led to a 125-year-old abandoned and forgotten construction tunnel—That, in turn, led to the basement of *Sacre Coeur Basilica.*

You are the best, Carlos. Now you'll earn your money— 2,500,000 additional Euros—4,000,000 dollars more— 14,000,000 Argentinean Pesos. And it will all be over in another hour.

* * *

In Front of Sacre Coeur

Buzzer, *Guy* and *René* sent Luigi and Luisa down the hill farther out of harm's way. The twins' job now was to keep a ground-level lookout for Carlos, while also keeping their noses tuned to the air around the cathedral. The two of them had proved in Argentina that they could sniff out a puma from a pretty good distance.

"If you smell him," Buzzer said, "give a shout on the radio."

Now, at almost noon, *René*, Buzzer and the two bomb squad experts crept back into the big church and headed for the basement.

"If he's really serious about blowing this place up," Buzzer said, "he'll have to plant his explosives at the base of the foundation. Otherwise, he'll just do a little damage to one wing or another. To bring this building all the way down, he has to destroy the piers sunk into the rock below."

* * *

The Old Construction Tunnel

Carlos slipped between the horizontal bars of an old, rusted gate that separated the abandoned construction tunnel from the basilica's basement.

Quickly and quietly he placed C-4 plastic explosive globs, each with a fuse, on several of the load-bearing concrete piers that held up the building. He wired the string of explosives in series and put an electronic detonator on one end. Once out of harm's way, himself, he'd trigger the first explosion electronically and the others would be set off by the first with a huge charge that would turn *Sacre Coeur* into a pile of gravel.

When he finished with his dirty work, Carlos headed for the back of the building. He'd let himself out a window and climb a long rain spout to the roof of the wing where his little flying machine would be waiting.

And he'd be off.

And richer than ever.

* * *

On the Street below the Basilica

"I smell puma, Luigi. He's here!" Luisa whispered frantically.

Luigi could smell Carlos, too.

He called on the radio, "Puma on the premises. We smell him. Be careful."

* * *

In the Basement of Sacre Coeur

Buzzer, *Guy*, *René* and the bomb experts had secretly watched from their hiding place behind some old wine barrels as Carlos had placed the explosives. With one snip of a pair of wire cutters, the two policemen had disabled all but the first glob of C-4 plastic. The others were no longer wired to the first one with the electronic detonator. Now they were working ever-so cautiously to disable the electronic detonator that they'd already pulled out of the C-4. One slip and they ran the risk of blowing themselves and the basilica up.

René spoke into his radio, "All observers, listen up. Carlos has left the basement and is likely about to be on the ground near the building."

Just then one of the bomb experts turned with a big smile and raised two thumbs up.

The electronic detonator was finished, and the two of them began packing the plastic explosives into a thick-walled lead box.

René continued, "Carlos' bombs have been disabled. He's leaving the building. Let's get him. Now!"

* * *

Outside the Basilica

Luigi and Luisa raced up the long stairs. At the top, Luigi grabbed Luisa by one paw and said to her, "That blue duffel bag on the roof. It belongs to Carlos, I'm just sure of it. Let's get up there."

He grabbed his radio and keyed the microphone,

"Buzzer, don't forget that blue bag on the roof. It must belong to Carlos. Luisa and I are going there now. Send *Guy* up to help us!"

Just as they rounded a corner of the building and looked up, they saw Carlos' tail slip over onto the roof at the top of a rain spout. This was the same section of the roof where they'd spotted the blue bag.

Luigi shouted into his radio, "Carlos is on the east wing roof. Right now. Where the blue bag was earlier this morning. Luisa and I are going up one of these tall chestnut trees so we can see over the edge of the roof."

Luisa was already halfway up the tree, with Luigi right behind her.

When they got high enough to see what Carlos was doing, they were amazed. If not awestruck. The big cat had almost finished snapping together an ultra-light with big blue wings.

Luisa grabbed the radio. "He's got a little one-pilot airplane on the roof, and he's almost got it put together. Hurry! He's getting away."

Just as Buzzer, *René, Guy* and the two bomb-expert policemen burst out a doorway onto the roof, Carlos started the little engine, revved it to full power and, strapped into a sling-like seat, leapt off the roof and into a sky already filled with hot air balloons, kites and random fireworks.

Buzzer started to key the microphone on his radio, but Luisa had beaten him to it. "Cincinnati and Dusty," she radioed, "Carlos just left the roof in a little ultra-light airplane. Get to that helicopter. Fast."

Dusty answered, "We're almost there. As soon as we

heard 'ultra-light,' Cincinnati told our taxi driver to get us to the helicopter *tout de suite.*[14] We'll be in the air in less than a minute. Keep your binoculars on him for us."

Now that Sacre Coeur *has been saved (or has it?) do you think Carlos will really escape? Where will he go in that little plane that's not much more than a big, motorized kite? Will Dusty and Cincinnati be able to pick him out from all the hot air balloons, kites and other ultra-lights in the skies over Paris? Should they shoot him down? Or just follow him until he runs out of gas? Carlos says he's headed for Munich. Do you think he'll get all the way there?*

---

14. Immediately, at once

Parlez Vous Français?
by Cincinnati

"*Excusez-moi,*"[15] but right now Dusty and I are trying to get a helicopter in the air, and trying to see if we can pick Carlos out from all the other flying machines of one kind or another in the skies of Paris on *Bastille* Day. So I don't have time for another lesson. Talk among yourselves. Here's a subject: "Smelly pumas on the run."

---

15. I'm sorry.

* Chapter 20 *
Pas de nouveau![1]

At Headquarters of the Brigade Criminelle

Buzzer and the twins had anxious faces. It had been more than an hour since they last heard from Cincinnati and Dusty, who were following Carlos' little ultra-light plane in their helicopter disguised as an air ambulance.

In their last report by radio, Dusty had told them they spotted Carlos when he broke free from the air traffic over Paris and headed southeast. "We're right behind him," she'd said. "We're staying 180 degrees in back of him on his same heading so he can't see us. And I'm sure he can't hear us over the noise of his own little engine."

Cincinnati had added, "It's a good thing we have a helicopter. He's probably going as fast as he can, but that's pretty slow. We just saw him pour more gasoline into his tank from a can, which he then tossed aside. We'll stay with him until he lands or runs out of fuel—one or the other."

---

1. Not Again!

Those left behind could do little but be grateful they'd saved *Scare Coeur* from destruction, foiling Carlos' ingenious plot and, without doubt, ruining the day for Count Frederic von Stuffel.

Buzzer keyed the radio tuned to the aviation frequency that Cincinnati and Dusty were using. "*Brigade Criminelle pour Ambulance aérienne numéro Un,*"[2] he said. "Do you read me?"

"I read you five-by-five," Cincinnati responded after a moment.

Relieved, Buzzer asked, "How's your fuel?"

"We're still okay on fuel," Cincinnati replied, "but I don't know how much Carlos could possibly have left. We've come a long way for an ultra-light." Then he said, "Here, talk to Dusty a minute. I'm getting some pretty fierce updrafts as we get nearer the mountains, and I need to fly this bird."

"Stand by, Buzzer," Dusty said. "Something's about to happen. Carlos is headed straight for *Mont Blanc*[3], and he's either going to have to turn, land or crash. Let me keep the binoculars tight on him, and I'll call you back in a bit."

Luigi and Luisa sat quietly in the corner of the room talking softly together.

"Well, Ma, I don't reckon that puma really did outsmart us. We had his plan in our paws fer two whole days. He hadn't got away yet."

"No Pa, he shore didn't outwit us. But he just ran faster

---

2. Brigade Criminelle to Air Ambulance One
3. Famous mountain on the Italian/Swiss/French border. In English, "White Mountain;" in Italian, "Monte Bianco."

at the end. Where you reckon he's a-headed now in that little putt-putt kite o' his'n?"

"Cain't go too fer, Ma. Thing don't hold much gas, ya know."

Buzzer wandered over, just to check what they were up to.

"Hello, there, Mister Barn Cat," Luisa greeted him. "My, my, you's a big 'un. Did ya bring Pa an' me any news from the airborne cat and the flyin' pig?"

Buzzer thought he might as well let them have their fun for the moment. He decided to see if he could make the little twins laugh.

"Well, Ma and Pa," he said, "Dusty and Cincinnati are following Carlos, and he's almost to *Mont Blanc* on the border with Switzerland and Italy. They say he's either going to have to turn, land or crash into the side of the mountain. Who knows which he'll do?"

That did it. Luigi looked at Luisa, who looked back at him. They burst into laughter and rolled around the floor, clutching their sides, snickering and snorting.

"Dusty's on the radio, Buzzer," *René* shouted across the room and over the din of the twins' laughing.

Buzzer hurried across to the radio. "What's happening, Air Ambulance?" he asked.

Dusty answered, "You're not going to believe this, Buzzer. You know the big tunnel under the mountain that connects France and Italy?"

"Yes, I know it," Buzzer answered. "It moves cars and trains through the mountain."

"Right. Well, Carlos just flew that little kite of his right into the tunnel. Dropped down on the top of a flatcar carrying logs into Italy."

"You can't take that helicopter in there behind him," Buzzer answered.

Dusty came back, "No, of course not. We're going to have to fly all the way around the mountain to try to catch that train on the other side."

Guy, who'd been quiet for an hour or more, interrupted. "We'll get the *carabinieri*[4] to stop the train as soon as it comes out on the Italian side. And they can seal off the tunnel until Cincinnati and Dusty get there."

"Did you hear that, Dusty?" Buzzer asked into the radio.

"Yes. Good idea. We're on our way around the mountain. Tell the Italians we'll be there in about 25 minutes."

René grabbed the microphone. "We're coming, too. We'll meet you on the Italian side in about ninety minutes."

Turning to *Guy*, *René* said, "Get our fast helicopter on this roof, *tout de suite.*"[5]

Guy smiled. "It's there. Waiting. I thought you might want to go after this Carlos."

✱ ✱ ✱

*Ninety Minutes Later—Between René's Helicopter
and the Air Ambulance in Italy*

"He's gone, Buzzer. He's not anywhere on that train. With the help of the *carabinieri*, we turned that train inside

---

4. An Italian word. The name of the Italian state police.
5. Quickly, immediately

out. We found his ultra-light all smashed up, right inside the tunnel on the French side. It looked like the train had run over it."

Dusty walked up. "Did you tell Buzz the one piece of good news?" she asked Cincinnati.

"If you can call this good news," the dancing pig said, "we found a Eurail timetable crumpled up with the ultra-light. It had several trains from Turin and Milan to Munich highlighted. My guess is he's headed for Germany—to Munich."

With a sigh, Buzzer walked over and handed Luigi his satellite phone.

"Call Dr. Buford and Bogart-BOGART back at the ranch, please. It's mid-morning there. Tell them we're probably headed for Germany. Carlos has slipped away, again."

Luigi took the little phone and looked at Luisa.

"*Une autre aventure!*"[6] he said.

"*Laisse tomber, petit frère!*"[7] Luisa answered.

Fin, pour le moment[8]

---

6. "Another adventure!"
7. "Let's go, little brother!"
8. The End, for now

Un million de remerciements[1]

Writing a 60,000-word book such as *Eiffel's Trifles and Troubles* requires several months of research, good French/English and German/English dictionaries, about 12,000 miles of travel, at least a dozen printer ink cartridges and four full reams of paper, a lot of thought and sweat, and—most importantly—the help and hard work of many people besides the author.

Special thanks to my sister-in-law, Barbara Arnold, of St. Petersburg, Florida, for actually pretending to be Carlos the puma for eight days in Paris. She helped set the flow and pace of the plot by whisking us around the City of Lights from one site to another, thus creating Carlos' plan on the ground. Thanks, BQ. Additional thanks to my brother, Jim Arnold, for researching places to stay in Paris, and things both to do and to avoid.

To the people at Eakin Press in Waco—thanks to you all. To Kris Gholson, publisher; Pat Molenaar, book designer; Kim Williams, cover designer; and Janis Williams, editor, for a precise job, turning a manuscript into a beautiful and useful book.

What can I say about Jason Eckhardt, the illustrator of the entire Cats of the C.I.A. series? Best just to say his work speaks for itself. Look at the illustrations, especially at the eyes. Then tell me you don't believe these characters are real. Thank you, Jason, for another great look.

---

1. A million thanks

Thanks also to my translator, Silvia Ambrosoli Konrad, who lives in Ecuador, for major help with the French language. I can navigate a bit in Spanish and Italian, but French, particularly pronunciation, is way beyond me. Silvia also translated the Italian book in this series, *Fred-X Rising*. Her native tongue is Italian, but she speaks and writes many languages—a true international.

Finally, each of my manuscripts is humbly submitted in advance to a panel of readers who invariably help to make the books better by catching mistakes and disconnects, and by making a variety of suggestions to improve the story. So thank you to all the following who read this rough manuscript two or three chapters at a time and contributed mightily to it.

Students
    Mariel Chun-shui Clark,4TH GRADE Irvine, California
    Brendon Keene, 6TH GRADE   Bandera, Texas
    Krystian Osbourn, 6TH GRADE   Bandera, Texas
    Erich Carmen, 7TH GRADE   Bandera, Texas
    Meghan Salley, 7TH GRADE   Bandera, Texas
    Wyatt Williams, 8TH GRADE   Bandera, Texas
    Emily Dianne Witmer, 8TH GRADE Bandera, Texas
    MacKenzie Errington, 5TH GRADE   Fort Worth, Texas

English Language Arts Teachers
    Krista Errington and Suzy Groff,
      Bandera Middle School, Texas

Adults
    Barbara Ivancich   Seattle, Washington
    Marion Woodfield   Seattle, Washington
    Cynthia Voliva   San Diego, California
    Lisa Gilbert   Houston, Texas
    Julie B. Fix, APR   Houston, Texas
    Mike Cooper   Galveston, Texas
    Avery Goodgame   Austin, Texas

✱ Un million de remerciements ✱

Ken Squier	San Antonio, Texas
Edward Stone	Dallas, Texas
Jim Haynes, APR	Dallas, Texas
Kelly West	Boerne, Texas
Jim Arnold	St. Petersburg, Florida
Barbara Arnold	St. Petersburg, Florida

To those who've never visited Paris—go! It's a beautiful city, clean and compact, with a great transportation system and more monuments than fleas on a camel. Pay particular attention to the world's most skillful pickpockets. They're quite adept. Yes, one or more of these clever operators did lift my wallet from my left front pocket somewhere on the Metro between Pigalle and the Left Bank. And yes, the *Prefecture de Police* did find it, intact except for the forty Euros in cash it contained.

C'est la vie.

As always, any mistakes you may find in this book are mine, and mine alone.

—GEORGE ARNOLD
Texas Hill Country
2011

Glossary and Pronunciation Guide

French Words and Phrases

The following phonetic pronunciations cannot be precise since French is pronounced so differently from the other Romance languages. However, French people, and particularly the Parisians, will appreciate a visitor's effort to speak their language, even if pronounced badly. Give it a try. And have some fun. Also notice how many French words are the same as, or similar to, their English counterparts.

English	French	Say It Like This
A		
a	*un*	a(n)
adventures	*adventures*	dhd-vehn-TEUR
again	*a nouveau*	ah-noo-VOH
airplane	*avión*	ah-VYOHN
airport	*aéroport*	air-oh-POHR
ankles	*chevilles*	sheh-vee-EH
April	*Avril*	avh-REEL
arms	*bras*	BRAH
August	*Août*	OOT
aunt	*tante*	TAH(n)-teh
auto racing	*course aux autos*	COHR-sah au ZAHTOH

| at your service | *a votre service* | ah VOH-treh sair-VEESE |

B

bacon	*bacon, lard*	BEK-on, LAH
banana	*banana*	bah-NAH-nah
barracks	*baraques*	bahr-AHK
baseball	*base-ball*	BAYSZ-bahl
basilica	*basilique*	bahs-eel-EEK
basketball	*basket-ball*	BAHS-ket-bahl
bathroom	*salle de báin*	sahl deh BAHN
beans	*haricots*	air-ee-COHT
bear	*ours*	OARSZ
beef	*boeuf*	BUFF
begin	*commence*	coh-MAHNZ
bellman	*groom d' hotel*	groom deh oh-TELL
belt	*cincture*	SAHN-teur
bicycle	*bicyclette*	bee-see-CLEHT
bird	*ouiseau*	wah-SZOH
black	*noir*	NOWAHR
blood	*sacre*	sah-CREH
blouse	*chemiselle*	sheh-mee-ZHET
blue	*bleu*	BLEH
boat	*barque*	BARK
boots	*bottes*	BOHT
bowl	*bol*	BOHL
bread	*pain*	PAH(n)
breakfast	*petit dé jeuner*	peh-TEE deh-zher-NAY
brother	*frére*	FRAIR
brown	*brun, marron*	BRAHN, mahr-ROHN
bus	*autobus*	au-toh BUESZ
butter	*buerre*	BURR

C

cake	*gateaux*	gah-TOH
candles	*chandelles*	shahn-DEHL
candy	*candi, bonbon*	cahn-DEE, BOHN BOHN
car	*voiture*	vwah-TEUR
caramel	*caramel*	cahr-ah-MEHL

cat	*chat*	SHAH
to catch	*attraper*	ah-trah-PAIR
cathedral	*cathèdral*	caht-eeeh-DRAHL
chair	*siège*	see-EHGZ
chase	*chasse*	SHAHS
cheeks	*joues*	ZHOO
cheese	*fromage*	froh-MAHZ
cherry	*cerise*	sair-EEZ
chicken	*poulet*	poo-LAY
chin	*menton*	MAH(n)-toh(n)
choir	*choeur*	CUER
chocolate	*chocolat*	shoh-coh-LAH
church	*église*	eg-LEESZ
city	*ville*	vee-AY
clerk	*concierge*	cohn-see-AIRZH
cloud	*nuage*	NUHGZ
coat	*manteau*	MAHN-toh
coffee shop	*café*	cah-FAY
it's cold	*c'est froid*	sest FROH
correct	*exact*	ex-ahkt
cougar	*puma*	POO-mah
Count (title)	*Comptes*	COMPT
cousin, male	*cousin*	coo-SAH(n)
cousin, female	*cousine*	coo-SEE(n)
cow	*vache*	vah-SH
cream	*crème*	CRIM
cup	*tasse*	TAHS
curiosity	*curiosité*	coo-ree-oss-eet
cycling	*aller en bicyclette*	ahl-LEH OH(n) bee-see-CLEHT

D

day	*jour*	ZHOOR
day before yesterday	*avant-hier*	ah-vahn-tee-AIR
day after tomorrow	*après-demain*	ah-PRAY deh-MAH(n)
December	*Décembre*	dee-SAHM-brah
detectives	*détectives*	day-tek-TEEV
dining room	*salle a manger*	sahl-ah mahn-ZHAY

dinner	*dîners*	de-NAY
dog	*chien*	shee-EHN
donkey	*ane*	AHN
dress	*robe*	ROB
driver	*chauffeur*	SHOH-FEUR

E

eagle	*aigle*	AY-gleh
ears	*oreilles*	oh-RAY-yuh
east	*l'est*	LEST
egg	*oeuf*	UFF
eight	*huit*	WEET
eighty	*quatre-vingts*	CAH-trah VEN
elevator	*ascenseur*	ah-sahn-SEUHR
English	*Anglais*	ahn-GLEH
escape	*escapade*	ess-cah-PAHD
eyes	*yeux*	YEUH

F

face	*visage*	vee-SAHG
Fall, Autumn	*Automne*	ah-TOH(n)
faster	*plus vite*	PLEU veet
father	*père*	PAIR
February	*Févrevi*	fev-ree-AY
fifty	*cinquante*	sahn-CAHNT
fingers	*doits*	DWAH
fire	*feu*	FEW
fish	*poisson*	PWAH-soh(n)
five	*cinq*	SANK
football	*le football*	leh FOOT-bahl
for	*pour*	POOR
forest	*forét*	fohr-AY
fork	*fourchette*	fohr-SZEHT
forty	*quarante*	cahr-AHNT
four	*quatre*	CAHT-reh
fox	*renard*	reh-NAHR
French	*Francais*	frahn-SAIS
Friday	*vendredi*	von-dreh-DEE

friend	*ami*	ah-MEE
front	*devant*	deh-VAH(n)
fruits	fruits	fruh-EE

G

German	*Allemand*	ahl-eh-MAH(n)
gift shop	*boutique de Cadeaux*	boo-TEEK deh cah-DOH
glass	*verre*	VEHR
gloves	*gants*	GAH(n)
goat	*chèvre*	SHEH-vreh
golf	*golf*	GOLF
good, well	*bon, bien*	BOHN, BYIN
very good	*trés bien*	tray-BYIN
goodbye	*au revoir*	aw-REVWAH
grandfather	*grand père*	GRAH(n)-pair
grandmother	*grand mere*	GRAH(n)-mair
grapes	*raisin*	RAY-szeh(n)
great	*grande*	GRAHN
green	*vert*	VAIR
gymnastics	*gymnastiques*	jim-nahs-TIQUE
Gypsies	*Gitans*	zhee-TAH(n)

H

hail	*grêle*	GRELL
hair	*cheveaux*	SHEH-voh
ham	*jambon*	ZHAHM-boh(n)
hands	*mains*	MAH(n)
hat	*chapeau*	SHAH-poh
hazelnut	*noisette*	nwah-SZEHT
head	*tête*	TEHT
helicopter	*hélicoptère*	ehl-ee-cohp-TAIR
hello (answering phone)	*alló*	ah-LOH
hello (greeting)	*bonjour*	bohn-ZHOOR
hockey	*hockey*	oh-KAY
home	*maison*	MY-soh(n)
highway	*autoroute*	au-toh-ROOT
hips	*hanches*	ahn-SZEH
horse	*cheval*	sheh-VAHL

It's hot.	*Il fait chaud.*	eel fay-SHOH
hotel	*hotel*	oh-TELL
How much does it cost?	*Combine ça coûte?*	com-bee-IH(n) sah COOT?
hundred	*cent*	SAHN
I'm very hungry.	*Je suis trés affamé*	zheh SWEE tray ah FAH-mee

I

ice cream	*glace*	GLAHS
in	*en*	EN
international	*international*	een-tair-nahs-oh-NAH(l)

J

jacket	*veste*	VEST
January	*Janvier*	zhon-vee-AY
job	*travail*	trah-VAIL
July	*Juliett*	zhu-YEA
June	*Juin*	ZHUEN

K

kitchen	*cusine*	cue-SZEE(n)
kitten	*petit chat*	peht-EE SHAH
knife	*couteau*	coo-TOH

L

later	*au nouveau*	ah noo-VOH
Let's go!	*Allons!*	ah-LOHN!
lightning	*éclair*	ay-CLAIR
lights	*lumiére*	loo-MYAY
lion	*lion*	lee-OH(n)
lips	*levres*	lay-vreh
little	*petit*	peht-EET
lobby	*vestibule*	ves-tee-BUEHL
lunch	*déjeuner*	deh-zhe-NAY

M

Ma'am	*Madame*	mah-DAHM
March	*Mars*	MAHRS
maroon	*bordeaux*	bohr-DOH

May	*Mai*	MAY
maybe	*Peut-etre, c'est possible*	PET-etreh, seh poh-SEE-bleh
midnight	*minuit*	meen-WEE
milk	*lait*	LAY
million	*un million*	A(n) mee-YAHN
Miss	*Mademoiselle*	mahd-mwah-moh-ZELL
mistake	*erreur*	air-EUR
Mister	*Monsieur*	meh-SURE
Monday	*Lundi*	awn-DEE
month	*mois*	MWAH
moon	*lune*	LOON
moonlight	*clair de lune*	clair-deh-LOON
morning	*matin*	mah-TAH(n)
mother	*mère*	MAIR
mouth	*bouche*	BOOSZH
museum	*musée*	moo-SZAY

N

napkin	*serviette*	SAIR-vyet
nave	*nef*	NEF
neck	*cou*	COO
nine	*neuf*	NUFF
ninety	*quatre-vingt-dix*	CAH-trah ven DEESE
no, thank you	*non, merci*	NO(n), mair-SEE
November	*Novembre*	noh-VAHM-brah
noon	*midi*	mee-DEE

O

October	*Octobre*	ock-TOH-brah
one	*un*	A(n)
orange (color, fruit)	*orange*	oh-RANZH
organ	*orgue*	OHRGH

P

pants	*pantalon*	pahn-tah-LOH(n)
parrot	*perraquet*	pair-oh-KAY
path	*chemin*	sheh-MEH(n)
pastries	*pastisserie*	pahs-tees-sair-EE

peach	*peche*	PESH
pepper	*poivre*	pwah-VRAH
pews	*bancs d' eglise*	bah(n) de-GLEESZ
pickup	*pickup*	PICKUP
pig	*cuchon*	cho-SHOH(n)
pillows	*oreillers*	ohr-reh-YEA
pistachio	*pistache*	peesz-TOSH
pizza	*pizza*	PEEZ-ah
planning	*projets*	Proh-zhay
plate	*plat*	PLAH
please	*s'il vous plait*	seel voo PLAY
police	*police*	poh-LEESZ
police car	*voiture de police*	vwah-TEUR deh poh-LEESZ
potato	*pomme*	POHM
prayer	*priere*	PREE-air
priest	*prêtre*	PREH-treh
pulpit	*chaire*	SHARE
purple	*violet*	vee-oh-LAY

Q

question	*question*	KWES-tyo(n)
quick	*rapide*	rah-PEE
quiet	*tranquille*	trahn-KWEE

R

rain	*pluie*	PLUH
raincoat	*imperméable*	ahm-PAIR-meh-ab-luh
raspberry	*framboise*	frahm-BWAHS
rats	*rats*	RATS
Ready?	*Prêts?*	PREH?
red	*rouge*	ROO-zh
restaurant	*restaurant*	res-tah-RAH(n)
rice	*riz*	REE
river	*flueve*	FLEUV
road	*route*	ROOT
room	*chambre*	SHAHM-breh
room service	*service de chambre*	sahr-VEESZ deh SHAHM-breh
running	*courrir*	coor-EER

S

sacraments	sacrements	sah-creh-MOH(n)
sailing	faire de la voile	fare deh lah VWAHL
salad	salade	sah-LAHD
salesman	marchant	mahr-SHAH(n)
salt	sel	SELL
sardine	sardine	sahr-DEEN
Saturday	Samedi	sahm-DEE
scarf	écharpe	eh-SHAHRP
sea	mer	MAIR
September	Septembre	sep-TAHM-brah
seven	sept	SET
seventy	soixante-dix	SWAH-sahn DEESE
sewer	l'egout	leh-GOO
sheep	mouton	moo-TOH(n)
sheets	drap	DRAH
ship	bateau	bah-TOH
shirt	chemise	shay-MEESZ
shoes	chassures	shah-SZEUR
shoulders	épaules	eh-PAHL
sidewalk	trottoir	troh-TWAH(r)
silver	argent	ahr-ZHA(n)
Sir	Monsieur	meh-SURE
sister	soeur	SEUHR
six	six	SEES
sixty	soixante	SWAH-sahn
skiing	faire du ski	fare deu SKEE
skirt	jupe	ZHEUP
small	petit	peht-TEE
snack	casse-croûte	cahs-CROOT
snake	serpent	sair-PAH(n)
snow	niege	NEHGZ
soccer	jouer a ballon	zhoo-AIR oh bahl-LOHN
socks	chausettes	shah-SET
Sorry, I'm sorry.	Excusez-mói. Perdonne mói.	ex-cue-zay-MWAH pahr-DÓHN-eh MWAH
soup	potage	poh-TAZH
speak	parlez	pahr-LEH

Do you speak French?	*Parlez vous Francais?*	pahr-leh VOOS frahn-SAY?
spoon	*cullière*	cue-YAIR
Spring (season)	*Printeps*	prin-TAH
stomach	*estomac*	es-toh-MAH
storm	*tempête*	tahm-PAY
strawberry	*fraise*	FREEZ
stream	*ruisseau*	REE-szeau
streets	*les roués*	lehs REU
subway	*metro*	meh-TROH
sugar	*sucre*	SEU-cruh
suite	*suite*	SWEET
summer	*eté*	ET-ay
sun	*soliel*	soh-LAY
Sunday	*Dimanche*	di-MONZS
sunlight	*luminère*	loo-min-AY
swimming	*natation*	nah-tah-SZYOH(n)

T

table	*table*	TAH-bleh
tablecloth	*nappe*	NAHP
taxi	*taxi*	tax-EE
telephone	*téléphone*	teh-leh FOHN
temperature	*temperature*	tahm-pair-eh-TOOR
ten	*dix*	DEESE
tennis	*tennis*	ten-NEES
thank you	*merci*	mare-SEE
thanks	*remerciements*	ray-mehr-see-MAH(n)
thirty	*trente*	TROHN-tay
three	*trois*	TWAH
tiger	*tigre*	TEE-greh
toast	*pain grillé*	PAH(n) gree-YAY
today	*aujourd 'hui*	oh-zhahr DWEE
toes	*orteils*	ohr-TEH(l)
tomato	*tomate*	toh-MAHT
tomorrow	*demain*	de-MAHN
tongue	*langue*	LAHN-geh
towel	*serviettes*	sahr-vee-EHT
tower	*tour*	TOOR

thousand	*mille*	MILL
thunder	*tonnerre*	tohn-AIR
Thursday	*Jeudi*	zhu-DEE
What time is it?	*Quelle heure est-il?*	kell air eh TEEL?
tiny	*petit*	peh-TEE
tomorrow	*demain*	deh-MAH(n)
toes	*orteils*	ohr-TAY
tongue	*langue*	LAHNGH
train	*train*	TREH(n)
truck	*camión*	cah-MYOH(n)
turtle	*tortoise*	tohr-TWASZ
twenty	*vingt*	VEN
twins	*gemeaux*	zhe-MOH
two	*deux*	DOOH
Tuesday	*Mardi*	MAHR-dee

U

umbrella	*parapluies*	pahr-ah-PLUEE
uncle	*oncle*	OHN-cleh
underwear	*souvêtement*	soo-vet-MAH(n)
United States	*Estats Unis*	es-TAHTS OO-nee
useful	*utiles*	oo-teel

V

vanilla	*vanille*	vah-NEE-yeh
vegetables	*légumes*	leh-GUHM
volleyball	*volleyball*	VOHL-ee-bohl
violet	*violet*	vee-oh-LAY

W

waffle	*gaufre*	gauf-FREH
wake up call	*reveil*	reh-VEAH
water	*eau*	OH
weather	*temps*	TAHMPZ
Wednesday	*Mercredi*	MAIR-creh-DEE
week	*semaine*	seh-MEHN
this week	*cette semaine*	set se-MEH(n)
next week	*la semaine prochaine*	lah seh MEHN proh-SHEN

last week	*la semaine dernière*	lah seh MEHN deh-NYAIR
welcome	*bienvenues*	byin-veh-NOO
Where are we going?	*Ou' allons nous?*	oo ah-LOHN noo?
white	*blanc*	BLANH
It's windy.	*Il y a du vent.*	eel ee ah deh VOHNT
winter	*hiver*	ee-VAIR
wolf	*loup*	LOO
words	*paroles*	pah-ROH(L)
work	*travail*	trah-VAY
wrists	*poignets*	PWAHN-yea

X

x-ray	*rayon*	ray-OH(n)

Y

yellow	*jaune*	ZHOHN
yes	*ouí*	WEE
yesterday	*heir*	ee-AIR
you	*vous*	VOO
You're welcome.	*De rein.*	duh-RIE(n)

Z

zebra	*zébre*	ZAY-breh
zero	*zéro*	ZAIR-oh
zoo	*zoo*	SZOO

What Happens Next?

- 🐾 Will Carlos make his way to Munich?

- 🐾 Will he learn that the Count von Stuffel talked too much?

- 🐾 If so, what will he do to the count?

- 🐾 Will the Cats of the C.I.A. and their friend Cincinnati the dancing pig catch up to him first?

- 🐾 What will happen at the Holiday Inn in Munich?

- 🐾 What of the "business" between Remy and the count? Is Remy a double agent?

Coming Soon from Eakin Press

München Madness:
Die Katzen of the C.I.A.

In this story, set in Bavaria (and including a 750-word vocabulary and pronunciation guide in basic German), the cats of the C.I.A continue their quest to capture Carlos and bring him to justice. Once again.

See how they get started on the following pages.

* Chapter 1 *
Making Tracks for *München*[1]

Le Bourget Airport—North of Paris

"*Le Bourget* tower, this is Sabreliner seven-zero-niner-niner-alpha ready for takeoff, bound for Munich."

Dusty, in the right-hand co-pilot's seat of Cincinnati's twin fanjet Sabreliner, *The Flying Pig Machine*, spoke English to the flight controllers at the small airport just outside Paris.

"Stand by, Sabreliner," came the reply from the tower. "We have traffic from *Charles de Gaulle*[2] and *Orly*[3] in the area. You should be clear in three to four minutes. When you depart, climb to 8,000 on a heading of two-zero degrees and contact Paris control on one-two-three-point-nine."

"Roger, *Le Bourget*. Standing by." Cincinnati, in the pilot's seat, answered the tower.

It was 8:00 P.M. in Paris, and the sun was nipping the

---

1. German word for Munich
2. Big international airport near Paris
3. Another major airport near Paris

western summer horizon. Cincinnati and Dusty completed their pre-flight checklist and idled the little jet on the taxiway.

Back in the cabin, a very tired Buzzer Louis was fending off his tiny orange siblings, the twins Luigi and Luisa.

"Tell us a story, Buzzer. Please," Luisa begged.

"Tell us about the little French poodle who won the sausage-eating contest the last time you and Cincinnati were in Munich," Luigi said. "That time when you shut down the big Vienna sausage caper."

"Tell you what, guys," said Buzzer. "I'm too tired right now to tell you that story. I need a nap. What if I put on the *Ma and Pa Kettle Go to Paris* movie as soon as Cincinnati turns off the seatbelt sign? Will that do?"

Luigi looked at Luisa. "Well, Ma, I 'spose if'n we cain't git no first-hand story, watchin' them funny yokels in Gay Paree would be second best, Ya think?" He was into his Pa Kettle routine.

"Shurr 'nuff, Pa. They's about as funny as you can git, I reckon," Luisa answered in her Ma Kettle voice.

The two had watched the movie Buzzer told them was the funniest film he'd ever seen—three times on their way from Buenos Aires to Paris, where they'd hoped to capture Carlos the puma, international terrorist.

Instead, Carlos had escaped at the last minute by strapping himself into a little ultra-light flying kite and launching himself off the roof of the *Sacre Coeur*[4] *Basilica* in *Montmartre*, a neighborhood in Paris. Cincinnati and Dusty,

---

4. In French, Sacred Heart

in a helicopter disguised as an air ambulance, had followed Carlos all the way to *Mont Blanc*,[5] where he'd flown the little aircraft into a big tunnel under the mountain, a tunnel that connected France with Italy.

Carlos had landed on a freight train's flatcar loaded with logs, but he never came out the other side of the tunnel. He just disappeared.

The *carabinieri*[6] had found the little aircraft near the French side of the tunnel, smashed as if it had been run over by the train. They also found a Eurail timetable that marked several train schedules from Turin and Milan in Italy to Munich.

"It's unusually careless of Carlos to leave a snippet of evidence behind," Buzzer had remarked.

Luigi said, "Or extremely clever to deliberately leave it behind to make us think he's headed to Munich."

Which was it? Carelessness? Or cleverness?

A call to Socks at C.I.A.—Cats in Action—headquarters in the White House basement had turned up the answer. Carlos's big Gulfstream G-550 jet had left *Charles de Gaulle Airport* bound south, but had changed flight plans in mid-air and flown to Munich.

So here they were. The four Texas cats and the dancing pig from Ohio, headed for Munich to once again try to corral that Argentinean terrorist, Carlos the puma.

* * *

5. In French, White Mountain. In Italian, Monte Bianco. A famous mountain on the border.
6. Italian state police

Eurail Station—Turin, Italy

Carlos thought he'd never been so tired in his life. As if the strength and endurance required to pilot that little ultra-light plane all the way from Paris to *Mont Blanc* hadn't been exhausting enough, he'd then had to cling by his claws to the bottom of a railroad flatcar in a tunnel for almost three hours until the dratted *Norteamericános, carabinieri* and *Brigade Criminelle*[7] had given up and left.

That delay, of course, made the freight train late pulling into Turin, and he'd missed the Eurail express to Munich. Now he'd have to take the last train, a local that would stop at every little hamlet through Northern Italy, Austria and Germany, and finally get to Munich at 4:00 in the morning.

Too, he'd somehow, somewhere lost the Eurail timetable he'd carelessly marked with schedules from Turin and Milan to Munich. *If they find that timetable, they'll know for sure where I'm headed. Or maybe they'll think I left it on purpose to throw them off the track.*

Carlos laughed. The "track" pun wasn't that good, but in his state of exhaustion, he would latch onto anything amusing, even only slightly, so Carlos locked the door of his sleeper compartment and climbed into the little bed. He covered himself with three blankets to keep in the warmth of his body heat so that it would soothe his sore muscles. Before the train left the station, he was fast asleep.

* * *

---

7. North Americans, in Spanish. Italian state police, in Italian. And Criminal Brigade, in French.

Back on the Taxiway—Le Bourget Airport outside Paris

"Sabreliner niner-niner-alpha, you're cleared for take-off," the voice of the air traffic controller gave the little jet and its cadre of crime fighters the go-ahead.

Dusty rolled the plane to the center of the runway, lined it up with the white center dashes and applied all the brakes. She pushed the throttles forward to ninety percent power, lifted her paw off the brakes and sent the Sabreliner screaming down the runway and into the evening sky.

Cincinnati watched his co-pilot in training with satisfaction. *She's really getting the hang of it. Wheels up at a thousand meters, nice turn to twenty degrees and a steady climb to eight thousand feet.*

"*Buen trabajo,*"[8] he said to her as he dialed the radio frequency to Paris Control. The two of them had made a deal. Cincinnati would teach Dusty to fly airplanes. And she'd teach him to speak Spanish. Both of them seemed to be doing well with their lessons.

Meantime, back in the cabin, Luigi and Luisa had their eyes glued to the television monitor. Ma and Pa Kettle had just learned they'd won a trip to Paris, and they were ecstatic. So were Luigi and Luisa, as they watched a very funny movie.

Before taking a nap, Buzzer Louis had taken out his secure satellite phone, turned on the scrambler and dialed his boss, Socks, in the White House basement.

"We saved the basilica," he reported. "Pulled the plug on Carlos' C-4 plastic explosives. No big bang. No damage at

---

8. "Good work," in Spanish.

all. But we lost him at the last minute. He's headed for Munich. That's where we're going right now."

He listened for a moment, then said, "That background noise? It's the twins watching an old black-and-white Ma and Pa Kettle movie."

He paused again. "It's 9:00 in the evening here—about 2:00 in the afternoon where you are. We should be in Munich by a little after 10:30. We'll be staying downtown somewhere near the railroad station. We're pretty sure Carlos is coming in by train.

He was quiet for a moment, then said, "Good. We'll e-mail you tonight when we get settled. And, yes, I think we still have plenty of Euros. Goodbye, for now."

As Buzzer finished his conversation with Socks, Luisa hit the pause button on the video player and turned to her big brother.

"Who speaks German?" she asked, "besides Luigi and me, I mean?"

Buzzer looked surprised. "Where did you learn German?"

"At Sister Mary Cannonball's kindergarten," Luigi answered, "Where else?"

Luisa added, "Well, duh, we live in the Texas Hill Country, Buzzer. Lots of people there speak German. We picked it up at school. It's pretty easy, really."

Luigi pressed the question. "Who else speaks German? In Cats In Action, I mean?"

Buzzer answered, "Only Cincinnati."

Luisa smiled a smug grin."Then Dusty doesn't speak German?"

Luigi gave her a high four. "Then I guess we'll just have to teach her."

Both kittens laughed hysterically. They loved knowing things Dusty didn't know. They could make her eyes twitch really easily by speaking German.

✳ ✳ ✳

On the Eurail Train – Stopped in Innsbruck, Austria

Carlos woke with a start. Something was wrong. What was it?

I didn't hear an explosion on my way out of Paris. I put enough C-4 under that church to make a big noise. Did it not work? What went wrong? The first eleven smoke bombs around the city went off, right on schedule. I've got to find a news channel to see whether Sacre Coeur is a pile of rubble, or whether it still stands.

He grabbed his iphone and punched up CNN Worldwide. *If Sacre Coeur is destroyed, it will surely still be on the news.*

What do you think Carlos will do when he finds out his plan to blow up the big basilica in Paris has failed? Will he conclude he was sabotaged by his own client, the Count von Stuffel, who may have said too much and given away the target? And what about Dusty Louise? Will her eyeballs twitch the first time Luigi and Luisa speak German? Why do you think she gets so upset when the twins know something she doesn't?

Other Books by George Arnold From Eakin Press

The Cats of the C.I.A. Fiction Language/ Adventure Series

■ **Get Fred-X:** *The Cats of the C.I.A.*—(2009)

Meet Dusty Louise, Buzzer Louis, Luigi and Luisa and Buzzer's best friend and C.I.A. contract operative Cincinnati the dancing pig as they take on Fred-X, catnapping owl who steals cats and tries to sell them into slavery. This first book in the series takes place in the United States where Fred-X is stealing cats in the Hill Country of Texas and flying them to Memphis every night. How will Buzzer and Cincinnati outsmart Fred-X this time? With a big surprise that gets him to promise to give up his catnabbing ways and head for Mexico to become a farmer or a taxi driver.

■ **Hunt for Fred-X:** *Los Gatos of the C.I.A.*—(2005)

Sure enough, a tiger never changes his stripes and a catnabbing owl has trouble giving up his dreadful habit, too. This time Fred-X is in *Chihuahua* in Mexico, where he's nabbing cats and flying them to the *Yucatán* to sell into the cat slave trade in Aruba. With the help of the Mexican national police, the *Federales*, the four Texas cats and the dancing pig from Ohio track the owl across Mexico. In the process they learn a little Mexican geography, history, culture and considerable Spanish. You will, too, with a 750-

word Spanish vocabulary and pronunciation guide built right in.

■ **Fred-X Rising:** *I Gatti of the C.I.A.*.—(2007)

The tricky Fred-X is up to his old habits again, this time in Italy and with the help of his German girlfriend Frieda-K and a greedy Cardinal from the Vatican. They're snatching Italian cats in the *Trentino* to take to a one-armed ship's captain in Venice to transport across the Mediterranean Sea to the cat slave market in Tunisia. The four Texas cats and Cincinnati track Fred-X down one last time with the help of a man with a wooden hand and a band of Greek stunt cats on motorcycles. In the process they learn some Italian history, geography, culture and how to speak the Italian language. You will, too, with a 750-word Italian vocabulary and pronunciation guide built right in.

■ **Tango with a Puma:** *Los Gatos of the C.I.A.*—(2010)

With Fred-X finally and firmly in the hands of the *carabinieri* in Italy and the *Federales* in Mexico, the cats of the C.I.A. turn their attention to an old nemesis, that infamous international terrorist, Carlos the puma. You see, Carlos has escaped from a dreadful Brazilian prison where he was sent four years earlier after Buzzer and Cincinnati tricked and captured him at a tango and wine-tasting contest in Buenos Aires. Now on the loose, Carlos returns to Buenos Aires where he plans to get even with the *Norteamericáno* cat and dancing pig. Our heroes set a trap with an ingenious plan devised by Luigi and Luisa to put him behind bars once again. In the process they learn a great deal about Buenos

Aires, Argentina, the Amazon River in Brazil and all of South America. Too, they improve their Spanish with another 750-word Spanish vocabulary and pronunciation guide, this time with more advanced Spanish as spoken in Argentina. Join the fun and you can polish up your Spanish, too.

■ *Eiffel's Trifles and Troubles: Les Chats of the C.I.A.*—(2011)
With the help of *Capitán Ramos*, shady captain of a 39-foot trawler, Carlos manages to escape from the headquarters of the *PFA—Policia Federal de Argentina*—by blowing up a corner of the building with C-4 plastic explosives. Socks, head of the C.I.A. in the White House basement, intercepts a ship-to-shore call from the South Atlantic that tips our heroes off to Carlos' next destination—France. They beat him to Paris, arriving in time to defeat his plan to blow up the *Sacre Coeur Basilica*, thus saving Paris from a dastardly terrorist attack. But Carlos manages to slip away by launching himself from the roof of the cathedral in a tiny ultra-light aircraft. Unusually careless, Carlos leaves behind a Eurail timetable that's almost sure proof he's headed for Munich. The Cats of the C.I.A. and Cincinnati visit the famous spots of Paris and learn to speak some basic French. So will you, because a 750-word French vocabulary and pronunciation guide is built right into the book.

■ **COMING SOON**—*München Madness: Die Katzen of the C.I.A.*—(2012)
Frustrated by Carlos's second narrow, last-minute escape, our heroes track him into Bavaria to put a stop to his

terroristic ways once and for all. The book will feature a 750-word vocabulary and pronunciation guide in basic German.

Adult Nonfiction

■ *Growing Up Simple: An Irreverent Look at Kids in the 1950s*—(2003)
 This international award winner, which critics compared favorably to *Tom Sawyer*, chronicles the almost unbelievable hijinks of a group of creative kids between kindergarten and high school—from 1946 to 1961—a time when it was still possible to grow up simple. Foreword by Texas icon Liz Carpenter. Winner of the Violet Crown Award from Barnes & Noble and the Writers' League of Texas as the best non-fiction book of 2003; the IPPY Humor Award from the Independent Publishers Association as the funniest book published in North America in 2003; and the coveted Silver Spur for marketing excellence from the Texas Public Relations Association.

■ *Chick Magnates, Ayatollean Televangelist, & A Pig Farmer's Beef: Inside the Sometimes Hilarious World of Advertising*—(2007)
 An extremely funny, yet completely factual account of twenty-five years inside one of the more creative ad agencies in the Southwest. However, the book is not about advertising or ad agencies, *per se*. It's a tribute to the power

of creative thinking and a business primer on the ground—where the rubber meets the road.

BestSeller: *Must-Read Author's Guide to Successfully Selling Your Book*—(2003)

The truth, the whole truth, and nothing but the truth about the role of the author in marketing his or her own books. For the writer who wants to be published and the published author who wants to sell ten, fifteen, twenty times more books. Accompanied by 90-minute, in-store workshops in bookstores and for writer's groups across the South.

Detective Craig Rylander Clover Mystery Series—with Co-Author Ken Squier

■ ***ENIGMA:*** *A Mystery*—(2010)

The lives of seven young girls in Austin, Texas, hang in the balance. Detective Sergeant Craig Rylander and psychologist Dr. Amy Clark race to find them against time and the pressures of an irresponsible, demanding press and self-serving politicians running for office on their backs. The *Austin Monster*, presumed kidnapper, has apparently grabbed them off the streets, leaving no trace, no clues. Will Rylander and Clark be able to solve the case and find the girls? Craig with his many years of no-nonsense investigating style, putting criminals behind bars; Amy with her perceptive insight into the violent criminal mind. And, if the girls are found, will they be dead? Alive? Or somewhere in between? The clock is ticking.

■ **COMING SOON—***UNDERCURRENTS: The Van Pelt Enigma*—(2011)

Guilt-plagued Austin Detective Sergeant Craig Rylander, disappointed in himself for failing to protect the innocent victims of an arson fire, cancels his much-deserved vacation to take on solving the arson-murder and a seemingly-related car-bombing that claimed five lives, including the newly re-elected district attorney of Travis County, two of her assistant DA's and a police technician. Rylander soon discovers that the force behind these tragedies is likely a gold-plated sociopath with unlimited resources who also heads a centuries-old worldwide assassination ring. Can Craig crack the local cases without getting entangled in a heinous international conspiracy? The F.B.I., C.I.A., and Interpol all scoff at the idea, but a confident Rylander pulls his team together and plans the investigation . . . as if this were just another routine case, which it definitely is not.

For More Information Visit the Author's Website
www.CIAcats.com

About the Author

Eiffel's Trifles and Troubles: Les Chats of the C.I.A. is the fifth book in the language-learning, international adventure series starring four Texas cats and a dancing pig from Ohio as secret agents working for the C.I.A.—Cats In Action— clandestine arm of the U.S. State Department headed by Socks, a gray tabby, and operating out of the White House basement.

In addition to the five Cats of the C.I.A. books, George has written two award-winning nonfiction novels, a how-to book for writers and authors, and an adult fiction mystery, all of which are in print from Eakin Press.

He began writing books after retiring from a 32-year career in marketing, advertising and public relations. For the last 22 of those years, he was president and chief operating officer of one of the more creative agencies in the Southwest— EvansGroup, Inc.

Today, George lives in rural Texas with his wife of almost 50 years. They have four children and five grandchildren, and they raise coastal Bermuda hay, dogs, cats and invisible goats. The four cats and two dogs featured in this book are all real, and all live with the author.

For more information, visit the author's website:

www.CIAcats.com